INISHBREAM

VICTORIA BC, CANADA

I visited a
Little Free
Library

VictoriaPlacemaking.com

Other books by Theresa Kishkan

FICTION
Sisters of Grass

POETRY
Arranging the Gallery
Ikons of the Hunt
I Thought I Could See Africa
Morning Glory
Black Cup

ESSAYS
Red Laredo Boots

INISHBREAM

a novella by
THERESA KISHKAN

GOOSE LANE

Copyright © Theresa Kishkan, 1999, 2001.

All rights reserved. No part of this work may be reproduced or used in any form or by any means, electronic or mechanical, including photocopying, recording, or any retrieval system, without the prior written permission of the publisher. Any requests for photocopying of any part of this book should be directed in writing to the Canadian Copyright Licensing Agency.

First published in 1999 in a special limited edition by Barbarian Press.

Inishbream is a work of fiction. Names, characters, places and incidents are the product of the author's imagination, and their resemblance, if any, to real-life counterparts is entirely coincidental.

Edited by Crispin Elsted and Laurel Boone.
Wood engravings by John DePol.
Book design by Ryan Astle.

Printed in Canada by Transcontinental
10 9 8 7 6 5 4 3 2 1

Canadian Cataloguing in Publication Data

Kishkan, Theresa, 1955-
Inishbream

2nd ed.
ISBN 0-86492-287-6

I. Title.

PS8571.I7516 2001   C813'.54   C2001-900132

Published with the financial support of the Canada Council for the Arts, the Government of Canada through the Book Publishing Industry Development Program, and the New Brunswick Culture and Sports Secretariat.

Goose Lane Editions
469 King Street
Fredericton, New Brunswick
CANADA E3B 1E5

For Jeremy Shanahan

An Invocation
to Saint Brendan

THEY EXIST ON THE ROUTE of great migrations. From high points on their island they can observe the plants, fish, birds and the human wanderers, all moving westward to some dreamed land. The northern diver, tired of flight, rests on the waves; the currents carry kelp aloft. These will all arrive on some far shore, a clump of themselves in a weary tangle.

And Brendan, you desired to leave parents and motherland, you set forth in a skin-covered craft, the hull formed and measured by your body, length of your forearms, distances between your knuckles, width of your palms. Notched sticks were employed. Your boatswain, a seabird, a black-footed albatross; your guide and your god, the polestar.

And the fishermen, Brendan, they were excited, unable to contain themselves. They relayed the following information: *It was a greatish currach, flying two sails as they did long ago, and by God it was a sight to behold, them ladeens aboard talking of a journey over the wild ould Atlantic, past the Faeroes and Greenland, and with luck they'll arrive at a new land, if ye can believe such a thing!*

You have shown them the guidance of the Great Bear and Orion (beloved of moony Artemis and the brightest constellation). These fishermen are your fair sons, fathered by your outpouring love for the old whore-sea and all skills of navigation.

THE BOOK OF THE GENERATIONS

I HAD NOT KNOWN about the islands. I'd thought the land ended suddenly and completely, the way land will, losing itself to the sea, and then only cold water and swimming things travelling the long miles to the banks of Newfoundland.

So I'd no thoughts of staying. The coast itself welcomed those on journeys, provided meals of brown bread and stout, but it did not gladly entertain the idea of settlers and refused growth of any nature. And it offered no empty houses, just shells of granite rock, roofless and claimed by birds, a few renegade badgers, some travelling folk who could stretch canvas temporarily over the tops to keep out a disapproving sky, a rain that would never stop. For no one approved in heart of the tinkers, nor of a wayfarer, stooped with a pack and a storyteller in my own small right.

No one told me that off the coastline existed a riddle of landforms, mysterious with oratories, old boats you'd dream to fix, protected species of birds, beasts, and sometimes poets who incanted through the days in stone houses of the ancestors.

It was a vet who'd given me a ride, his destination the smug town at the extremity of Connemara.

– You're looking for somewhere to live? Mostly you'll find only holiday rentals, and you'll pay very dear. But why don't you try the islands, or at least try Inishbream. It's close.

It was. You could see it from the Sky Road when you knew where to look. Just a few visible houses, the lichen-growers, and not a lighthouse to be seen, only a lanky protective Mother of Jesus, whitewashed yearly by a fool who'd go, and the rocks. There is a legend told of the Children of Lir: they rested on those rocks in the form of swans. And years before or later, Saint Brendan the Navigator sailed past in a currach of skins, smeared with animal grease to keep out a threatening sea because everyone knows a duck will not be cold or pulled under when the oil is still on its feathers.

I remember there was not a ferry, the island too small for a regular schedule and a dock of large proportions, the necessity of a hired captain and a Bord Failte office with maps and brochures (though you'd find one in the town, with a telex that never functioned). The vet drove me to the strand, and I waited where the land ended, on the edge of a typical field defined by stone walls, no sense of geometry, shapes awry and scandalous.

And where the field ended, the stones began an untidy descent to the sea. The man who was Festy Kenneally (for Fechian, saint of the buried chapel on Omey Strand) was riding the tide in, the bottom of the currach scraping. I went to meet him, and I helped him pull the craft across the strand, anchoring it finally with heavy rocks, laying the oars to rest.

– May I ride across with you?

– I must first be bringing the turf down.

We did that, brought down sacks of sweet fuel, the fruits of several weeks' labour on the bog and delivered by Miceal O'Gorman, an Eyrephort farmer with a van. Smelling the turf, I remembered riding down the Westport road past the acres of acrid earth, wondering at the crops of such a place.

– Do you burn the earth?

– We do.

My arrival startled no one. There *was* the house of someone's dead mother, was there not, and it should be lived in, with the roof a new one. A woman yet! — but a lover of boats and sea, and *she can pull the ould currach like a man,* Festy assured them after we'd rowed in tandem to the quay, myself hiding the blisters. We made the boat fast, and then I was shown the house.

It faced north, the northern sea, marred only by lichens and the slow passage of snails over the damp wall. There were dead ashes on the hearth. Three calves who lived permanently out the door. An elderly, confused dog who smelled the special smell of burning turf in an abandoned chimney, who was lured by it, and who claimed me. A broom of broken corn husks.

The first wind whistling down the chimney, dropping a blackened bird on the hearth, frightened me, and I began to see the wisdom in the words of a man who'd told me as I gathered my rucksack from Festy's boat: *Ye'll be wanting a man to keep ye busy in that house when the storms come.* The dog, uneasy as if the wind were a banshee, began a moaning as unearthly in its own way. That night we walked, the dog and I, under the cold moon and through the weaving gazes of the islanders. The dog ran fitfully, cautiously indicating his route and possessions, and it came to pass that the sand at morning tide was a calligraphy of his prints, that the stones of Inishbream were rank with his urine.

— What is your work, I asked.

— We are farmers of the sea and thin earth that covers these island stones.

I looked and saw only thistles and nettles, a few potatoes, no trees of corruptible fruit. I saw only thorns and a sea full of eels.

— What will I eat?

— He has given us herbs of the field.

And they were there, if you'd only notice, a funny weed you could chop as a salad, nettles for soup, wild garlic, a small secret bed of cress in the marshy ground of the long-ago bog.

Though I came wanting only the isolation of tides, it seemed inevitable to wed. He was the someone with the dead mother, his parents had lived in my house, coupled silently in the bed I slept in under the Sacred Heart, producing their eight and a few washed away. His mother swept the same floors with a similar broom, leaning partway through her work to watch the terns on the rocks;

the door frame where I stood with binoculars was worn soft with her watching. Sean came, a dog or two winding around his feet, bringing gifts of turf or potatoes, as his father had and as *his* father had, all the days of the island since Cromwell. The dogs joined the elderly keener (silent in company); the front of the fire was a twitching complexity, a grunting tribe of sleepers. We did not talk much or well. Instead, he brought willow pots to mend, smelling sharply of lobsters and dogfish guts. Sat, twining nylon string through and around the woven wood, mending and renewing. I learned to knit the oily wool of the southern islands, making rough cables and designs in the silence. And a photograph of the parents hung stern-faced above the mantel.

— Would you like tea?
— I would.

A ceremony of necessity. His mother wept from her grave, expecting a cousin or local colour at least, and this one will never stay, O my grief! The father stared to sea from his grave. But the others were agreeable enough.

— Long as she works, that's all we could ask.

At first I dreamed of whales, heard them circling in the hollow of the sea. I saw grey whales, I remember, at Wickaninnish, a whole pod of them heading south to calve off Baja in the Sea of Cortez; there was only me on the beach to see. I woke and wanted to tell Sean, but he'd gone out to his lobster pots at dawn. When he came back, I told him, Sean, there were whales, I dreamed a host of them circling the island, it was lovely, as though they were telling us something important.

– Why would ye dream such a thing? Tis a quare business all right. We never see whales, though yer man with the fish van says a frame was found on the sands near Claddaghduff, all white it was in the sun, unskinned like an ancient currach. And that is all I know of the whales.

Case closed, shut tight as a cockle. Then he gravitated in the usual way to the shore to fill a bucket with sea water to store the lobsters in until collection day. They'd wait in the scullery, rattling their claws against the metal. I have never known such a world in all my life, where the caged sea frets and cannot bear to be absent from any part or thought of the day, where the boat remembers the living beast it took its skeleton from, the shape of leviathan locked at its core, where the megaliths brood and claim the island.

I spent a good long time walking the shore. I wanted to discover something. Mairtin O'Malley found an explosive on the west beach, and there was a notice on it saying: DO NOT TOUCH. NOTIFY AUTHORITIES IMMEDIATELY. He phoned from the post office, all the others there and listening, speculating about the possibility of the IRA. *Was there not a car hidden in a turf pile on the wild boreen across the bog linking Oughterard to the Westport road, and didn't yer woman send something from every pint to the boys in the north?* The Garda came by special launch and took the thing away. He wore gloves and touched it first with a broom. Mairtin felt cheated, and his children were angry.

– Ye mean ye let him just take it?
– Aye.

I saw things I could not carry: a boulder pale green with algae and scrolled with lichen; a pool so small you could cover it with your hands, but filled to the brim with little weeds and no doubt amoebas; the long path of sunlight leading to the mainland. But I've never found anything worth keeping in my life. The pebbles I take become dry and dull (*Whatever did ye choose that one for?*), the grey thing a distant cousin of a jewel seen in wet sand. The sticks must be burned, no matter that they lie on the shore like reptiles sniffing the wind. Once, when I lived near the Pacific, I saw the whales go by, enormous and dignified. No one else was there to see them. But you cannot display or prove a memory.

This is the way the generations begin. There weren't trees to link a family to, you could say they were all forced from the crevices of stone like crabs brought to the light. Miceal Walsh the elder, possessor of a tin whistle, a head full of airs, "Finnegan's Wake" and "Flanagan's Ball." Miceal the younger, husband to Margaret so long in the grave (barren-wombed as she was), husband to Bridie. Bridie Walsh, mother of six named for the saints, bare-footed, the youngest still in the red petticoats of the islands.

– It is so the faeries will not know whether they are male child or female and will be too confused to take one so.
– Oh.

And there was Sean, son of Padraig and Moragh, brother to the seven. Padraig, deceased but alive in the twilight memories; Moragh, deceased; the seven now departed to the marriage beds of a southerner, a northerner, a traitor and a slut. That accounts for four, and no one talked about the remainder.

Mairtin the father. Mairtin the son, half-witted but a visionary. Brother to Triona, Declan, Paddy Joe. Hawk-nosed brother to the petrel, the grey goose.

– Does Mairtin Og ever talk?

– And sure what would he say? Where he's been to tell us or done to spin to a tale worth our listening?

Festy Kenneally, a trammel-netter, a drifter on tides, a distiller, with bones for the weather and a taste for the poteen. Kathleen Clancy, a bearded virgin, possessive of a butter churn, a wireless. Her competition, the crone, professional keener and something of an oracle. And the sundry, an assortment of sainted children, men of the sea's kin, the dogs, the knitters, a healer, the quiet breeding seals.

THE GREEN FIELDS OF CANADA

THE HOUSE WHERE THE DROWNED MAN lived has been empty four winters. Before I ever came, they nailed the door shut, boarded the windows. All the whitewash has flaked, has gone to the wind.

I am told again and again of the tragedy, its impact.

His was the only body not found. The other three washed up on strands from Clifden to Aughrusmore, carried in the current north or south. I did not see them, I lived somewhere else then, but I know where they are now: in simple pine boxes sunk deep into earth on the island's western reach. The crosses are Celtic, are granite, are engraved with their names.

But the man whose body knows no rest. He is somewhere in the passage between island and mainland. After storms I half expect to see him on the rocks below my house. I found a seal there once, cold and alone and rotting in the sun.

I have walked by his house late in the night. There are never lights, and so I know the sea keeps him even then, will not let him dry by the hearth (it has been stone cold so long), will not let him sleep (he will have circles of fatigue under his eyes).

I have been ferried across to the island at midnight. The water has been silent and black, the oars cutting deep and breaking phosphorescence. I imagined him following us, wanting only to be seen and drawn up, wanting to be washed clean of sea moss and brine.

The other three wait for him there in their beds on the western point. They wonder why he has been so long.

– Will ye never come home, never come home?

Miceal plays to the twilight, a hunched old piper. His sad notes haunt the island, and slowly doors open. We all come out to stand, hands on the stone walls, our bones echoing the tin whistle's quavering, married to wind and lyric of terns. Miceal wakes the moon from her sleep in the ocean. He brings home the night-swimming fish, the last boat of the day.

The island is a boneyard in its own way. Bullocks, in pieces on the dunes, lie hidden or else reveal themselves to walkers: a fine slab of clavicle, a fragment of tooth. What I find, I line along the mantel or upon the windowsills. All day they are silent and ornamental. At night they are given flesh and form, become populations of the dark, searching for food or a mate. Storm petrels, their beautiful claws. An otter.

And the fishermen are careful with all bones of the

catch. To burn them or to allow dogs to gnaw the brittle spines would bring bad luck. I have told Sean stories about the rivers full of salmon on the northwest coast of Canada, and he does not think it strange that those fishermen bless the ribs as they toss them to the breeding streams.

– And do new ones grow from the bones so?

– I think so.

And I tell him a salmon song: *Hung-e, tunga, kwul-lo, kain-tla, ta-wit, shin-kin, is-la, the eye of your knee knows the coming of spring.* Our own knees pull us to the quay, and we lay out the mackerel nets, we mend them.

In the beginning, the other fishermen were afraid I would bring bad luck by coming to the fishing ground. Women didn't and that was that. For months I waited daily, with the other women though not one of them, for the boats to return. Sean wore a cross on his neck, blessed with holy water by the crone who lives in the final house, her windows facing west. And I waited, each day going on forever, the sea refusing the vision of return. Then two men died in a boat off Lettergesh, the boat sinking and the men drowning with their hands still holding the oars. Lettergesh, only a few women remaining, huddled back into the mountains after the wake, small with loss, unable to forget.

And so my help was needed, and nothing more was said about luck. This is the season of fruition: the mackerel running in green shoals, the lobsters filling the pots, spider crabs weaving themselves in like offerings and not refused by us or any others. Packy Conneely, the fish dealer, comes to the strand to meet the catch.

And we rise each morning before the sun has a chance (or is defeated by mist), pull out to Errislannen in the currach. The first net we bring up is alive with dogfish, and I kill them for bait. Sean pulls on his own, as I cut the raspy, speckled bodies into pieces. Then we bring up the pots in pairs, and as they break the surface of the sea, we see the mass of crabs, their claws waving in supplication.

– Grab the back legs if ye can.

I can, and I bring them out, one by blessed one, to lay in boxes, covered with shawls of sea-wet sacking to keep them cool. Sean, baiting the pots, steadies the currach from time to time with an oar. Our anchor is an island stone, falling to the bottom like a prayer.

✠ ✠ ✠

– Will ye tell us a story, something about where ye come from?

All of them, settling around the hearth for a story, the poteen on the table, the women wary-eyed and knitting.

– Have ye a story to tell us, then, woman of Sean?

I'll tell a story about leaving and returning. It's about fishing ports and animals, it's about coming of age on an island.

– What island? Not the Great Blasket, where ye say ye've been?

– No, not the Great Blasket, that's someone else's story.

But an island all the same, positioned on the rim of the Pacific, an island of rainforests and mountains, a town laying light over the Strait of Juan de Fuca all night long. North of San Juan Point, on the western coast, the open water crashes against beaches and settlements, and the sea-bottom rocks with the wrecks of galleons and trawlers.

— And have ye pukauns there?

— We haven't. But there are ghost ships off Hansen Lagoon, brigs and whaling barques that have drowned on the offshore reef, their holds full of useless blubber and pelts. There are skinless sea otters crouched by the salt-stinging tide, bleeding into the sea, saying, We will let in no others, saying, We will refuse to breed if this is our fate.

— And is that near to where ye was born?

— I was born in a later century on the southern tip, in a hospital not far from Oak Bay. I spent my early years watching for pirates, learned to navigate the seasons by a wild sea, learned tides and the fathoms of winter, all the ports of entry. I had an ordnance survey map pinned to my wall, and it read like a litany: Nootka Sound, Kyoquot Channel, Carmanah Point.

— And how would ye get there? By currach, as we do?

— No, the ferries sail every hour on the hour, and planes land every day, their wings silver as a heron's back and beaded with rain.

— Planes! Ye'd never get a plane to land on this ould rock, though once a helicopter did.

— The city I was born in is not unlike an Irish port

town, Cork or Galway or even Dublin, though smaller. Gulls and tourists strut all summer on sidewalks leading to the sea, steamers blast arrivals and departures all day and night. My father, as I have told you before, was a sailor as a young man, and on Sundays he would take us to the docks where we would walk the tar-thick piers. Bright flags of the foreign ships, sickles and stars, hemp ropes, boxes of slick white-bellied halibut. My father wore a seaman's sweater from Spencer's Store, and he knew the most elaborate knots.

— Aye, being a sailor, like.

— Yes. And sometimes we went aboard the ships. I remember lockers with bare-breasted women glossing the doors . . .

At this point the women's faces flush and they frown, and I wonder if I'll ever forget that I know about anatomy, shall I ever learn to hide in the dark fear of sin like the circle of women who look from one to another and won't meet my eyes. One woman glares like a harpy at her knitting. *She* would never let me forget.

— I remember canvas kit bags shoved beneath bunks. On the deck, I stood at the prow like a skinny-kneed figurehead, and I watched to see if I could tell which man had a wooden leg, the inevitable sign of piracy. I watched the tremor of muscles under striped t-shirts. For a few years we lived close to the sea, and I slept on a captain's bunk built into the attic of our house. A telescope leaned out of the gabled window, and I watched for whales, for frigates sailing homeward. Up there, I could hear the ghostly crews of the wrecked galleons, I swear it. All night I heard the drowning song over water . . .

— Aye, ye can hear that here some nights.

— and as I grew older I heard the words of the keening, the language of grief, the rhythms of loss. Polished bones I saw through the telescope: the ghost crews parted the fogs in lifeboats, layers of algae coating their skulls.

— John Joe O'Malley over at Ballyconneely said there was an algae stuff on Mickey Keane's body when they found it after those months it spent in Mannin Bay, and that's God's truth, I tell ye.

— Waters around that island teemed with life, every sort of life. I used to pretend I was a diver, borrowed my brother's snorkel, saw kelp swaying in the undercurrent, saw plankton and the hunting fish among the weeds. I parted the weeds: Dungeness crabs scuttled off sideways. And sometimes you could see the fishermen unloading boxes of the trapped crabs, and if it was a festival or a Sunday, maybe they would boil them right on the docks in big cauldrons, cracking the claws open for the pale meat, leaving the beautiful mottled backs.

— Tell us more about yer father. The sailor.

— Well, he walked with a rolling gait, as though he could not believe he was landlocked. He took us to beaches where he sat looking to China across the sea . . .

— Fancy that!

— while we splashed under the sun. I would rise from the waves, a sea-born daughter of Venus. My father heard the mermaids singing.

– Aye, we call her Maighdean Mara here.

– And we gathered bark on these beaches for our stove at home, and soft glass and bits of shell. Rubber devices that I thought were balloons until I was smacked for trying to inflate one. No one explained. It tasted of something left long in the sea. Salt of life. Sometimes there were detergent bottles tossing through the kelp, and once I saw a walrus with its eyes plucked out. There were fish bones from the natural deaths. Waterlogged trees, limbless and smooth, escapees from the north coast booms. We cut these for firewood.

– And we've only them hollow bramble stalks, not worth the collecting. Ye'd be better off burning scraws ye can find on the back bog.

– There were car trips up the island, and I learned a kind of physiology, mountains running in a backbone down the centre of land, the matrix of granite . . .

Sean whispers to Mairtin the meaning of these strange words in the terminology of his almost-forgotten sojourn at boarding school: Well, it means natural life, living things. A science, Mairtin. And I wish to myself that I could learn to forget my vocabulary, to say the right things in the right words. Sometimes I feel as though I speak a foreign language.

– and my father taught me a secret bestiary of island animals: black bear, the salmon-poacher . . .

– I hear they've caught ould Eamon Joe Kelly poaching sea trout near Derryinver.

– whitetail, the bark-eater; elk, the star-catcher (I heard

the sound of locking antlers in his words). The ark of our small boat in the mountain lakes rang loud with the syllables he taught me (vertebrate, mollusc) and the tent was haunted with fossils of another time, glacial or Jurassic.

— Now yer getting beyond us there. But thank ye all the same. Now maybe Festy'll sing us a song. I am thinking "The Green Fields of Canada," lad.

— Aye, now let me think. That's it. Yes.

> *My mother is ould and my father quite feeble,*
> *To leave their own country it grieves them full sore,*
> *And the tears down their cheeks in great drops are falling,*
> *To think they must die upon a foreign soil.*

And after a few more songs in Festy's low, peculiar whining voice, we leave to go back to our houses, the dogs following and the stars alive on the island for light.

The black bull did not want to enter the water. Three men in a currach, two rowing, one holding the halter rope and pulling, a dog urging the heels of the bull to go forward, the watchers tossing seaweed at the big rump and shouting at him, Go on, go on, ye ould thing.

I watch, myself, from the house on the cliff. Our three calves bawl to the morning, to a long-gone mother and this great bull who might have been their father as bulls are that way. A morning alive with this one's reluctance, the frenzied multitude of dogs who gather to assist the first brave mongrel, who has by now been kicked in the ribs by a winging hoof and who has retreated in humiliation.

When the bull finally swims, urged by God knows how many shouters, he goes with the tide. The men are at the mercy of his strength, and he draws them toward the island quay. He rises out of the water and up onto the ramp. The men are shouting, the one with the rope is pulling hard, pulling harder, and that bull is slipping back down the weedy ramp and into the sea.

This time he swims behind them, bellowing. It is a half-mile to the low tide mark of the mainland, and he swims behind the black currach, herding it into the land.

We all row over later. The day is only barely defined in the mist, close and grey and ideal for bartering, as Peter remarks. We gather our shopping baskets together. The men are wearing the mended jackets, smelling strongly of mothballs, that they save for town and Mass at the Kingstone Chapel. The women have flattened their heads with kerchiefs, the patterns having not a thing to do with their dresses, and black shawls. The men pull caps flat to their own skulls, and everyone is in Wellingtons, town shoes in precious bundles beneath their arms.

On fair day, the town is always a hive of cattle and drivers, and this one is no exception. The streets are thick with the excited shit of the cattle, the heated language of the buyers, the exultation of the sellers. And stout floats out of the public-room doors, sweetish and encouraging to any deal or contract. The shops are full of island and mainland women, alike red-faced with vodka (*For the arthritis, ye know*) and defensive of their purchases (*It's a soggy ould cabbage, God knows, but it'll do for the soup, and who's fussy at these prices?*). In Kelly's pub a ceili band is hard at reels in a corner, the fiddler's bow slicing the air wildly and threatening the crowd who move too close; the uillean piper is pumping hard as he's worth, pausing between sets for a drain of his Harp. A drunk farmer, pleased as a tinker with his transactions, sings of the transportation of the boys of Mullaghbawn in the opposite corner.

Some island cows, previously brought to the mainland ahead of the amorous bull, are standing among the townies, fat and proud as the devil, bringing a good price and they know it. The islandmen are thrilled with the Christmas of ten-pound notes.

The afternoon fills itself easily with the generosity of drink, sweets, the finest meal Eamon Kelly can produce. (Turkey, mind ye, whispers Agnes, and he usen't to serve but the finest of sea trout.)

By twilight we are ready to make our way to the strand, to ferry ourselves back to Inishbream. Our feet are weary with the accomplishment of strutting and jigs in unfamiliar shoes; we are bound for the island, our blood homing and keen for the bed.

✠ ✠ ✠

A web of life, spun from the sea's fine silk, sargasso, mist and the sheaves of barley knotted by Himself and mended yearly by the fishermen.

That ugly basking shark. It was such a quarrel to bring him in, the sea sulky and unwilling to help, the currach small in a tower of waves, and the thing itself crowding against the boat, crowding, battering, bleeding into the sea, a misery of red, and the sea sympathetic to its creature. The towing out to open water, much stronger he was than the bull, even dying. Bringing him back was no triumph but a blessing.

– We thank ye, Lord, for what ye have given.

And his liver, when opened, yielded gold in the form of precious oil.

A web of life. Tentacles. The foot of a gannet.

The stones were not dolmens or cromlechs but cyclopean, bald, and the chanters themselves. The island was ringed by them, protective, irrefutable. The houses were built of their offspring, the fields' grey crops were inspired by their image. In the sweat of thy face shalt thou eat bread, till thou return unto the ground; for out of it wast thou taken. Ringed with stone, stunted by stone, made barren by stone, buried in stone (the graves a passage through the stone heart of Inishbream). And the rain, strangely mineral in its own falling. A knot of stone toads at the bottom of the well.

A web of life. The wintered nets hanging over a cliff, anchored by a megalith, the incarnation of His mystery.

– If I made ye a cap, would ye wear it? That ould one of Sean's does not become ye.

– Of course I'd wear it. The mornings are cold enough, that's true.

So the aunt made me a hat, pale oily wool that she had spun, then knitted, neutral cables and paradigms, row upon row of her memory.

– Ah, I cannot give ye the pattern (when I asked). Ye cannot do it by pattern. Ye just know when to make a cable, when to make a knot.

– I'd never know.

– Aye, but ye was not born here.

☩ ☩ ☩

The mail comes one day only, on Tuesdays, and the island tenses, is restless all the morning, waiting.

Sean expects nothing. And so he rows out to the lobsters alone, armed with baits and his mended pots.

Not many boats will go out on a Tuesday. Things get done in the homes: a dusting of the eaves, smoothing of thatch. (*Ah, ye cannot leave it bunched up like that. I will stay to fix it so.*) Floors are scrubbed with rough salt, bread is made in a low bastable. And I am busy to pass the time, tending to the calves, bringing sacks of turf up from the quay with the dubious help of an aged and stubborn donkey. The shore is dark with mouthdown currachs, humped into the sun like slugs.

– Don't expect it before two at least.

I hang the quilt out in the rare sun to air. We shall sleep in a fragrance of wind.

– That's only Mairtin you hear, not the mail boat.

I set pans of bread in the coals to bake.

Voices at the quay. Peter, back from a moment's fishing, talks to Festy about the possibility of crayfish in such weather at Carrickarona.

Two o'clock takes its own sweet time arriving.

Messages come from another world. My father writes to me about a trip to Alberta, at one time his home: "We buried my last brother yesterday in the family plot in Edmonton. I drove to Drumheller after the funeral and discovered that nothing much had changed there since we left in 1934. Saw dinosaur displays in the museum. I often looked for remains myself when I walked back in those hills as a young boy, but I suppose you'd have to dig a long way or be awfully lucky to find anything worth keeping. They'd all be buried deep. The wind is constantly changing the topography. And I visited Julia's grave. My sister. You never knew her. She died before even I was born and they buried her in the Drumheller cemetery. I went to the Sturgeon River where my school friend drowned so long ago. They never did find his body."

My father's archaeology. Burials, bones, the prairie wind. I write by return post of my new life on an island: "Father, I found a long curving bone, a dolphin rib, green with the sea, quite pitted by exposure. And a rudder from a sailing ship. These waters are wild, you'd want a sturdy craft. There are always dead birds on the shores, terns, petrels, and once an albatross, the claws neatly folded, the eyes pecked out. And Father, I've dreamed twice of an ocean voyage, a great ship surrounded by a host of birds and the dolphin following, silver-backed in the green grave of the sea."

The mail comes one day only. After the boat departs, having left its sack of post and carrying our epistles away, the bachelors gather in groups on the quay, toothless and talking about boats and disasters, politics and potato blight.

And they watch at the edge of the sea, the copulating sea (someone's old genitals, the rough white foam); they watch for a goddess, a hag, they wait for a salvation.

THE BOOK OF THE CHRONICLES

THE BOOK OF THE CHRONICLES, illuminated as it was by the endless and inbred families of fisherfolk, with the rough boats, the curious fish, marginal decoration of thatching days and the ricks of corn, the most common embellishment a curling, vine-drawn I: *iota* (gk.), from *yodh* (Semitic), meaning "hand", and now an abbreviated form for incisor, a variety of titles, the chemical iodine or inactive, the mathematical symbol for imaginary quantity, for island, for Inishbream. I, the qualifying noun.

And I am to remain childless. Something about biology, genetics (*a science, Mairtin*), though once there was a hope but then an ending of late bright blood. I knew about cycles and seasons, the way of a woman with a man, the rooted mandrake. Knew about the necessity of binding oneself to earth and stone with the young, their thin limbs forever bound to the island of their birth.

— It is because she will go out in boats with the men. Not right for a woman, and in trousers yet, with the cap of Seaneen and her hair underneath. Ye'd never know she was a woman. It's unnatural, like.

— And ye've heard, of course . . .

The tongues forever knitting the stories over tea. When I sit among the harpies with my clumsy cables and impure wool, I am always given the china cup of the guest. Never crockery, like themselves, homely and plain brown, but always the china cup of the stranger, my name engraved in the common-room silence. Readable, though in another dialect.

But I am learning the art of storytelling, of simplicity, the necessity of kennings and the harp-shaped caesura.

— What will ye tell tonight? Something about, let's say, a journey, something about Canada.

— Well, I could tell you a story about leaving and returning. My father's job took us away from that island I told you about earlier, away to Nova Scotia for several years. I remember it as a time of snow, and then summers spent exploring the East. A hole in a cliff in Gaspésie where a seabird crouched from the wind, a gannet or a gull. The great trapped lobsters waving their claws in restaurant aquariums . . .

A settling back, a lighting of pipes, the brand of burning turf on the fire.

— Now yer telling us something we know, like.

— the long vowels of the natives. Then, when I was ten, we changed coasts. Pilgrims of summer, lifting our taproot from the stunted Maritime soil and beginning the journey toward the West. High tide on the Bay of Fundy, waves, certain rocks, these I remember; and from salt to fresh to salt again I collected relics: stingray cartilage on a New

Brunswick beach, a smoothed Great Lake pebble, salmon ribs at the Fraser's mouth. We began by knowing the journey's end, a knowledge of permanence after a makeshift season.

— What about the place ye left?

— We left a city citadel, a common like Stephen's Green in Dublin or even Phoenix Park, controlled parkland with a semblance of wildness. There were fishing villages, similar to Cleggan or Roundstone, but they were called Hubbards, Herring Cove, Prospect, names that fall like fish into nets, and fish as well, the same fish you have here because the ocean was the Atlantic. Tides opposing but the water the same.

— Ahh . . .

— In the forest near our home at Rocking Stone I had often walked the dog, and once a man pulled his trousers down in front of us. The dog wasn't interested in the muscle hanging limp, looking like a small dead weasel. That is something I never told anyone. I'd thought he was the keeper of the forest and that he was somehow making us welcome.

Flushed faces, the men interested (*So she knows what one looks like . . .*), the women embarrassed (*Hussy!*).

— We left my grandmother's house on Chestnut Street, a house of gables, dark wood, a piano injured in the 1917 explosion in Halifax Harbour, blue Chinese ginger jars. There was a stern sepia grandfather, there were two girls who were never young, who never smiled, twists of iron hair wrapped round their heads. My mother said, This one is your Aunty Helen, and this one is myself. I could never quite believe her.

— Aye, it is that way sometimes with the photographs.

And Sean is looking deep into the fire, remembering the first judgement of the parents above the mantelpiece.

— We left. It was not until Fredericton that I was sure we'd actually go and not turn around to return. My grandmother was too old to transplant; we left her there sitting by her photographs. We'll come to visit, there are planes, it's only a few hours, we said. She was weeping out of sightless eyes, rocking her pain in a carved oak chair. I used to hold her hands and trace the blackened veins into the flaps of her wrists. We'll come to visit, we'd said. When we didn't, she died. My mother flew back, only a few hours, to touch my grandmother's hands, the holes where her eyes had been.

— And who did ye have to keen? asked the crone, herself a mistress of the death peal.

— We had ourselves, our relationship to her. And myself, I was the daughter of the daughter, reading of pioneer women launching their canvas wagons onto roads that all led west.

— Ah, like the tinkers then. Festy, would ye ever put another lump of the ould sod on the fire?

— I remembered the island in the West, of course, and I studied my father's maps. The names of the places were often Spanish or Portuguese, those nations claiming a foothold on the land in the beginning; or the names were Kwagiulth, Salish, born of the older time, called into being by the land and her offspring: Qualicum, where the dog salmon run; Chu-an, facing the sea. I was the daughter, alone in my place in our station wagon, thinking of a home in the West. We had our utensils for the journey and a canvas house wrapped up in a bag. We carried our photographs with us, impressed upon our retinas. There was one I looked at for a long time: my grandmother, my mother and I, arms braiding us into a single plait, but something not quite right. My mother and I are looking into the lens of the camera, my grandmother's empty sockets are staring wildly into space, an explorer with no sense of location.

— A plait. Fancy that! Kathleen keeps a thin plait of her dead mother's hair inside that gold locket she wears on her neck.

— Days we travelled a grey length of road, and we stopped like the faithful at stone cairns marking battles or discoveries. My father's voice intoned our history. In Quebec . . .

— Aye, that's where all the Frenchmen are trying for independence. Sure and don't we know about the struggles here.

— they spoke an unfamiliar music, the "Frère Jacques" of early school the only French we knew. Their hands were quick as light, arms trembling like a weathercock West. In the tent at night, all six of us lay in rows like cells inside a honeycomb, breathing. On the prairie, my eyes grew parched. There was no water. Rivers of mud went snaking through fields and irrigation pipes to nourish the pale crops. That gravity was a constant pull as the oceans fought for us. My mother turned to me, said, Do you remember the train trips to Wolfville for the apple festivals? And the pipers up from Cape Breton in their kilts? But Mother, that was long before my time . . . Yes, I suppose it was your grandmother I went with, but it seems like only yesterday. When you were a girl? Yes. And I wondered, could my grandmother see the blossoms in her mind? Has she always been blind? No, but she was then. Oh. And the music, of course she could feel that, running in a shiver down her spine.

Miceal the elder nods vigorously. Aye, ye can feel that stuff singing in yer bones, and that's His truth.

– My mother's nostalgia and excitement for a dead time made me uneasy, and I wondered at our connection. Blood, I supposed, but not our souls. But then she told me a story: that she'd dreamed as a young girl of bridling a Sable Island pony, riding the Atlantic home to Lunenburg County, and I had dreamed myself of a similar ride after seeing the ponies in a *National Geographic* magazine.

– Another island! And where does this one lie?

– It's a crescent moon of a shape lying southeast off Nova Scotia. The ponies from sinking Spanish galleons swam there hundreds of years ago, have managed to survive, breeding hardy and foraging for surf grass, galloping all night over dunes and the days surrounding a lighthouse.

– What about yer father? The sailor.

– Well, he remained neutral. He'd actually been born in

Drumheller, far from the Atlantic or the Pacific, and it wasn't until he was eighteen that he went to the sea at the end of World War II. So at heart he belonged to the prairie, too, and his uncle, the oldest man I have ever known, carved for us a land-going dinosaur out of hickory root. Its mouth was open, showing teeth and tongue, and two chips of amethyst were planted in its eyes.

— Get back to the journey.

— Well, we drove through a long string of prairie grain towns, clusters of houses, elevators for the dusty crops, wheat-coloured people tight-lipped in the general stores where we drank cream soda, and everywhere the dust, the chaff, the distance. You could stand and look for miles and not see the end of your vision. In cities like Brandon or Regina, there were fountains that sprayed our faces and felt like breakers if we closed our eyes, but they did not smell of salt. All those Historic Site Ahead signs my father noticed. He told us stories of uprisings ...

— And sure don't we know about uprisings? Isn't Pearse's cottage where he learned the Irish just over in Rossmuck?

— of Riel and Dumont, and he took photographs of my brothers and myself lounging on restored wagons and mastodons.

— Not real ones, surely? Yer codding us there.

— No, I mean reconstructions. You know. Or else fossilized. I don't remember much of the detail. I was anxious to take that ferry to Swartz Bay and to stand still at the prow until we arrived. In the past, on short trips away from Vancouver Island, we had pretended we were the first explorers watching the Gulf Islands grow out of the mist, hearing the first croaking of the ravens, seeing the original waves breaking over the backs of killer whales. But we stayed a long time in Alberta. My father was a young boy, showing us where he'd cycled miles on Sundays for ice cream. He took us to the badlands. I remember not much colour but an eerie wind. And we were taken to a game farm to be shown sleepy-eyed animals. I was the impatient one, felt like a tiger in a page-wire field, camera-snapping tourists waiting, breathless, as she rose and stretched, then started pacing.

— A tiger! I've not seen even a picture of one, but in the books they tell us them tigers and such are related to the cats. My Boots and Festy's Frisky. Striped, though, if ye can believe such a thing.

— I can, Bridie. And my father's sisters cooked for us. The food he grew up on, the pirogy and holopcha, seemed as exotic as quail's egg or caviar. He talked the whole journey of the Sturgeon River. A boy he knew dived from the bridge, never came up. When we went there, I imagined his corpse and the others it spawned resting among the weeds.

— Aye, the way ye think that the oars will touch the drowned man whenever we row out near Fahy.

— Yes. And when we went back to the aunts' house that day, my father drank whiskey with an uncle, and they looked through the yearbook of their thirteenth autumn. That young man on the Sturgeon's muddy bottom. He smiled. He will never look older than that. He never knew about the war to come that we, as children, had to learn to imagine. My brother, older though younger, showed me pictures of shaved heads and pits of bodies. I, younger though older, knew about Hitler.

– I've read about that monster. Like Cromwell, he was.

– It did not take long, once we left Alberta, to make our way to the coast. We camped in the Rockies, thinking only of grizzlies. In our dreams they flattened our tent and ate our dog. Then the road, stretching itself like a rattlesnake . . .

– Ye won't find a snake in all the counties! Saint Patrick himself banished them all from the face of Ireland a very long time ago, and they're afraid to this day of returning.

– through the Okanagan, passing stalls of peaches, early apples, jugs of cider and cherry wine. Finally through the tunnels, Devil's Elbow and Hell's Gate, along the highway to the ferry terminal at the mainland's edge. The ride across took one hundred minutes . . .

– That long? Is that a fact? We can row on a fine day from the island to Eyrephort in just twenty minutes. In a currach yet.

– and we walked the decks, pretending the boat was our own, pretending we had never been away. We flung the images gathered on the journey to the Strait, where they sank down to the sea's bleak heart. We lived, after that, in a great house of distance. My mother wept in the night for snow, wept like a rain that would not stop. My grandmother rocked all night in her dreams. My father fished the rivers for trout and steelhead. He would not fish in the Sturgeon River, I remember, but stared down from the bridge to its depths. We lived near the sea in the house with the captain's bunk and telescope, and I took my secret vial of Atlantic Ocean there, flung it into Gonzales Bay and waited: for the explosion, for Poseidon, for a goddess to rise from the waves. Stepped back in disappointment, and as I left I looked once behind me to see the ghost of a girl coming home across the ocean, her hands resting on the weedy mane of her pony.

— Ah, I understand yer meaning, though ye'd be best off to simplify in the odd instance. But yer telling a better story now all right. Will ye have the poteen?

— I will.

And someone piles more turf on the fire, the knitters race each other through the rough wool of their days, dogs twitch, Miceal extracts a tin whistle from his pocket and summons a reel from its heart.

☩ ☩ ☩

I am walking the island's circumference, past the megaliths and cottages. The sea is alive with currachs, the current and her lover undertow. What I have found: blue mussels, hooked mussels, barnacles, the skeletons of sand dollars, sea snails, tube-building bristle worms, sponges, starfish, mermaid's hair and rockweed, bladder wrack, the crystallized salt around the edges of rock. I have found curious marks on the sand. I think they must be hieroglyphs, the whole intertidal zone literal with their message. Figures, rituals, wildlife. I think I have found the language of the universe.

— Sean, who would have done this and what does it say? (trusting his knowledge of the island's strange events and visitors).

— What are ye meaning?

— This (pointing to the intricate narrative).

— Oh, that. Well, it is only the feet of the top-shell, that spiralled lad ye may see there (pointing to a conical shell just beyond). It is that they feed upon the algae, grazing from bit to bit like a cow may.

I look. The figures decipher themselves, and I see their meaning, not as symbol or the unfolding of allegory, but as the passage of sea animals, quiet, determined and possessing no urgent need for language.

Sean goes back to the picking of carrageen, the queer gelatinous moss which he dries, then sells to the Breton at Cleggan. I follow, though not in his footsteps that imprinted themselves like fossils in the sand.

— But these, Sean? (pointing to the circular carvings on the exposed stone). We might call these petroglyphs in Canada.

— And what is a petroglyph?

— Well, the original people carved pictures directly into rock . . . daemons, monsters, gods, events, the turning of the seasons . . . and it was, I guess, their record of the world.

— Aye, like the carving on the dolmens. But these here are only the marks a limpet will make with his pull. And if ye watch long enough, ye may see them return after their feeding. They will always return to the scar they have made. It is like a home to them so.

Mist lies over the island, potent and mysterious, like God's breath. Although there is famine in the sea and the dogfish raid our nets, tangle themselves, are trapped gaunt and anguished when we find one, something is prolific: protozoa, creating themselves out of brine and the drowned man's sperm, creeping ashore, shaking themselves free of the sea, then splitting, multiplying. They simply exist, mindless, without the cursed memory of falling, wandering, waiting, sinking. They are flesh-eaters at the dawn of evolution, speechless but whole. Every day we are thus renewed, given freely, without pain, without cost, new life to be among us.

There are pale beaches of coral sand, strung darkly with the dead weeds. I walk them endlessly, alert for news of the world: a bottle, an explosive, a book of the saint's voyage enacted on the edge of the Atlantic, a waterlogged crate washed from the deck of a ship.

In those windy cottages, the stories age. Outside, a well runs dry. Pots rise empty on their bleach-bottle floats, the hay rots under the rain's assault. And they stand, all of them, on the rim of the chopping sea, straining to the tide, pulling in the nets of morning. World without end, amen.

IRISH MIST

LISTEN. There were *weeks* when the sun refused us. At first I thought I could never live in such a place, but then I learned the sweetness of the Irish mist, how it enveloped you and numbed you to any real action or consequence. And you wandered in it, your hair jewelled, and you let yourself drift in great imaginings, where the ruined castle on the coast was made whole and you lived there, where the beached hooker was yours and you mended it. Occasionally a stranger, even more so than yourself, came to find something out. Were there corncrakes, nearly extinct on the mainland but thought to exist on the islands, where a scything farmer would watch out for the nests? There were. Would anyone sell a house to a foreigner for a summer place? They wouldn't.

I never knew whether to believe the tales. A feud so great the Senate was involved. A fortune hidden in the oldest man's bedsprings. They sounded fine if you heard them wound out of a mouth around a pipe and punctuated by bird cries.

But there were days when I wanted something more to happen. I'd arrange to be left off on the strand, or I'd row myself over in an available currach, and I'd walk the northern portion of the Sky Road. It was nice to use the muscles the mist had allowed to become soft and to really stride out the few miles to the Westport road. Once there, I knew the dilemma: north to places unknown and even a friend to visit in Mayo; south to Clifden and the monotonous streets; back the way I came. I went north once. Sometimes south for an unexpected afternoon in the town, rummaging in the magazine shop for something to read and once finding *The Tree of Man*, having tea in the lobby of the Celtic, talking to anyone who talked to me first. Often back the way I came, walking down the Sky Road's vistas into soft rain and the fuchsias.

At home, they wanted to know about my day; you could never row away unseen or return unheralded, if only by dogs. And Sean was always a little hurt, not knowing the need to ever leave except maybe of a Sunday when the football matches were played and replayed in every Clifden pub and the beer was particularly well drawn. If you could last long enough there was a dance in the hall at half-eleven, some pop band off-key on the improvised stage. Or you could always find an after-hours, the owner peering out at you first as you knocked on the bolted door, recognizing you and squiring you downstairs, where it seemed the whole town, including the Garda, had gathered for a last drink that became another and another. Maybe someone had a fiddle or a tin whistle, maybe it was even Miceal, and there'd be good crack and all your favourite tunes in the smoky, illegal air. Coming back was spooky, the rowers miraculously sober (though you'd not support them in a court of law) and a few singing and no lights to be seen west, but you knew you'd find land and your home and with luck the last of a fire.

And listen, I want to say what I felt. Sometimes I could not believe my arrival and the subsequent stay. I'd come for a holiday, not a life. And then I was charmed by the stones, believing them holy and omnipotent. And then I felt a prisoner, chained to respectability by the watching and the talk, barred from island life in its true estate by the fact of my alien blood (three parts Romanian, one part Scot). I was happiest walking alone on the north end, where you could look for miles beyond Slyne Head and see nothing but the restless sea, maybe a boat on a lucky day, and often even the horizon was invisible. If the wind was down and your own ears good, you could hear the throaty seals on Carrickarona. There were things to be found though you could not lay claim to them: threads of rope, fishing floats (and not the magical Japanese glass ones which you had in your old home, no, these were rusted metal), a boot that made you wonder, a little piece of wood with Mandarin stencilled on it. The landscape made me sad in a bittersweet way. I was overwhelmed by the pale colours, the mists and the stones. Music, when released from Miceal's whistle, as it was nightly, or the wireless, was obviously bred out of the land, sad with hardship and lost love, soft-edged by the weather and keening like the wind. I felt lured by it and to it, though I knew my kinship was assumed and not organic.

THE BRAND

— SAINT BRIGID OF THE MIRACLES, I ask to be forgiven.
— But it is not to me that you should come with your confessions...
— My Lady, the priest comes over the sea in a miraculous way with wafers and a flask of bitter wine. He arrives in his mysterious robes, and his neck is thick with beads and a cross. He talks of obedience, of fear and trembling. He threatens. He does not come to listen to me.
— And what is your sin?
— I have wanted more than I was given. I have sat on stone I came seven thousand miles to find, and I have cursed its coldness. I have been sad at the sea's edge, looking west to another land. I have cursed any acceptance of the fourteen images of the doe-eyed Christ. I have found all devotion difficult.
— Your sin is the common sin of an exile. The brand of the traveller is impressed upon your breast.
— My Lady, it is because I have lain with him.

☩ ☩ ☩

There is no one to blame. That day began simply as a journey to the town. I was alone, having rowed myself over the waves to Eyrephort Strand, anchored down the currach with stones, planted my oars in the sand. I wanted to walk. A brilliant day in Connemara under the sun, and the seven miles of hilly road unravelled before me through a glory of fuchsia and marsh marigold. The camp of the travelling people bloomed under one hill like an exotic hybrid. Two caravans, orange canvas, bright clothing planted in the gorse, a sorrel mare haltered to a stunted tree, a wisp of smoke.

– Good morning to ye. It's a fine day and that's His truth. Will ye take a cup of tea?

– I will.

A cup of potent tea, paled with cow's milk. I could see not a cow in the tinkers' proximity but knew Paddy Bourke's herd grazed nearby. A cup of tea, offered in the enamelled cup of the gypsies.

– Ye'd not be Irish, I'm thinking.

– I'm not. But I'm living on Inishbream.

– Ah, the one ye can see from Eyrephort.

Children swarming in the gorse, dogs, a few men smoking, indolent, against one caravan. I drank my tea.

– I'll be leaving now. Thank you, the tea was nice.

One man struggled himself free of the group. I'll go along with ye.

A hero of a man, dark, and blue-eyed as the devil. We

walked quickly, matching stride, not talking until we reached the last hill. I could see the town's spires, Catholic in the centre, Protestant (and lower) on the edge, sticking into the sky. And far below, the currachs of Inishbream preyed upon the lobsters of Carrickarona; the coral strands of Ballyconneely startled my eyes.

— Yer no man's woman, I'd say. (out of the blue, and sharp as a knife).

— Why would you say that?

— Ye've the look of a mare no man could ride, all impatient with ropes and angry. Ye've a sad look in yer eyes. His own eyes pierced me like the fangs of a serpent, the banished serpent of Patrick's wrath.

Below the rise, he led me through the broken hedge, through the tangled remains of a castle garden. By a little stream, we lay down together. There were no eyes of a dead mother to watch nor the eyes of a priest to condemn. I heard the tide breaking below, heard the far-off barking of the seals.

I went back alone through the vines, parted the hedge, stepped onto the narrow road.

Christopher, Christy, saint of the wayfarer, saint of the traveller.

When I returned along the road from the errands, the tinker camp was deserted. The halter of the sorrel mare was hanging empty on the tree.

(The brand of the traveller there on my breast.)

— Had ye a good day?

I was putting away the parcels, filling the kettle.

– I did. It was a nice day for walking the Sky Road.
– Peter says there's the tinkers up by Paddy Bourke's.
– I saw them. They gave me tea.
– Ye'd be best off not taking from the tinkers. Tis a strange life they live, always moving, never settling.
– And you, Sean? Do you never think of leaving? There are so many parts of the world to see, so many things to do . . .

He was silent. Then: It is only when the great flights of geese go over us when we are out in the boats, so many of them that ye could not count, and they have no thought of alighting, only of flying forever across the sea, it is only then that I want to go off. They would not know things the way we know them, it would be the wild places they'd be wanting, and would ye just think of the trees, the fishes, the openness they'd be knowing that we'll be dead and never see.

Those were more words than I had ever heard from him, forced from the soul of him, flung from the tongue of him into the room like wild misplaced animals, scattering, hiding, first in the inglenook, then in the eaves.

– And you? Are ye unhappy here?
– Seaneen, I love Inishbream. You know that.
– Aye.

And then I put aside my wool, the ribs and imperfect cabling of my residence, and I went out walking. There was a new, new moon, thin as a thought, and only the nightjars calling. I walked to the crone's house, the farthest house, and she had made a brew of comfrey leaves *(for the arthritis, ye know)*, and offered me a mug, my own ache as physical, though not located in the joints or sockets and easily treated.

— It is a wonder the faeries don't take ye, walking as ye do under new moons, hair unbound and not even that ould dog to protect ye.

— He won't stir after the six o'clock news, I'm afraid. But are there faeries on Inishbream?

— There are strange things that happen, as is the way in any place of their seeing. The sorrows. Aye, and there is a ring of stones of the south commonage, and do not take it upon yerself to step inside. That is where the cows go to spill out the dead calves. They are helped by the faeries, like.

— What about the stones themselves?

— Ah, the stones are a quare lot. The one that is the colour of heaven, lapis, it will cure the melancholy. The stone of the East, the sapphire, it will make the mind pure, it will make peace.

I saw the traveller again, on the second Thursday of the month, the cattle fair day. He was driving some skinny heifers along the Sky Road, and I was cycling, my shopping basket hanging from the handles of the borrowed bicycle.

— Ye look like ye've ridden over the waves.

— No, it's Seamus McGrath's, the man who has the holding above Eyrephort.

— Tis a fine day for the riding.

— Yes, isn't it? Will you sell all the heifers?

— I will try. But tis the same in every town, no one

wanting to buy fair from a travelling man because they think tis stolen or diseased cattle they will be getting. Sure and these are the local cattle I have bought fair and square. But they'll argue and complain that it's cheating them I am up to.

Those eyes. And the hands of unusual ways and knowledge.

-- Christy, I'll be riding on now. Perhaps I'll see you in the town.

And I did, I saw him in the square of deals and bartering. Eamon Kelly was assessing one of Christy's heifers, running a hand over the bony hock, examining the nostrils, fixing a suspicious eye on the rectum (*no worms that I can see, but these tinkers are a crafty lot*).

Not many islanders had come for the sale. I'd a list of shopping and errands (*Would ye ever pick me up a box of tea? the mail? see yer man in the post office about me pension cheque?*) which I proceeded to do in my own sweet time, pausing to talk to the postmaster, pausing to take the sun with some of the town lads by the statue of some hero of the Troubles. Then: Will ye have a drink? and Christy was there, and then we were walking to the little pub at the bottom of the market street.

– Did you sell all the heifers?

– I did. And I took less than their worth, which is a right joke for a tinker. But I am not one to wait around a town to feed the beasts up to look swell and fat. I bought them thin local and I meant to sell them that way, too. I am thinking a beast is more than the flesh on its bones so. And we are ready to move on.

The Guinness was good. Thick, warm, black as the devil's heart. The pub we took our pint in was an alchemist's workshop of bottles, fruit, sweets and the alchemist himself, Mossy O'Malley, divided in half by a white apron and a man to mind his own business. A few drunk farmers. A smell of dung and the sweat of man.

– What of yerself? Will ye stay on so?

I did not know how to answer, how to say I am as happy here as I'd ever be, which is not particularly happy, but a part of the sea and land if not the people and content enough. O that.

– Ye seem a traveller, too (when I did not answer).

– I am. I mean I was, have always been, but I'm not now. Or, at least, I can't be.

– Ye've a man then? Ye seem not to be a woman with a man in her heart.

– He's not in my heart. But he doesn't mind. We get along well enough.

– I am thinking yer fooling yerself there. A man wants always to know where he is with a woman. But, now. Have ye the children? Ye seem not much more than a child yerself.

– I'm old enough all right. But no, I haven't a child, and perhaps I never shall. It just doesn't seem to happen. The islandwomen mind about that, of course. They mind terribly. People marry to have children, they think, and there is something spiritually wrong, morally wrong, with the woman who does not have a child within the year of her marriage. Or, God knows, perhaps she is barren and not blessed by Saint Jude. And maybe they're right in my case. But I love fishing, and if I had children I wouldn't be able to go for lobsters. I'd hate having to be in the house all day, it would drive me mad. Fishing is good work, Christy, even on the roughest days.

– Ye do not love him.

A statement. A fact of life, and death as well, because I think I shall enter the grave having loved no man on earth. I did not say this to Christy.

– Let's have another drink and then I must go.

We did that. And then we were walking past the church spires and over the hills, pausing to embrace by a thorn tree but not lingering, and finally we were at the camp of the tinkers. I walked my bike and Christy walked beside me, his hand resting on the empty saddle. It touched my back, entered my hair and held the back of my head gently.

– If ye liked, ye could come with us. There's room in the caravans, no one minds another.

– Where are you going?

– We will be going north, to Sligo, where some of the others have preceded us. There are the ceilis all summer, and my father is a fiddler. We shall be going around to them, to make a few quid, like. There's good crack all around and a chance to see other country. We'll maybe be going to Donegal after that. Now that's fine, with the wind and the wild sea and a chance to turn the horses out on the moor where there aren't so many farmers to complain.

– No, I guess I've chosen Inishbream and I'd better stay.

Then we were at the border of the camp, and he was looking at me with those eyes and asking with them Will ye come? and All I could give you, and I was mounting the bike like a difficult horse, and I was riding away, away, and I was gone.

– Seamus, here is your bike and thank you for lending it.

– Ah, it's there in the byre whenever ye need it, and yer welcome to it.

I dragged the currach down to the sea and loaded in the parcels, took up the thole-pins and the oars. The ride across was rougher than I was accustomed to meeting, the currents difficult and a wind rising. The currach lugged in the tempest of sorts, and my shoulders ached, the sweat of my brow stung my eyes. At the quay Sean met me and we made the boat fast.

– Ye were a long time. Ye must be tired.

– A little. The crossing over was difficult.

– It is not good for ye to cross alone. I have said that. Ye never listen. The next time, I'll row over with ye and we can arrange a time for yer return, or I'll watch out for ye so ye will not face the rough passage alone.

– We'll see. Many lobsters?

– Nineteen.

– A good lot?

– Aye, and there's some big ray and a black sole from the bottom net.

– Good. Let's have our tea.

We walked up the boreen, over the hard earth and the stone wall. As we passed the cottages, I delivered letters, tea and the pension cheques. Twilight, and the turf fires were catching nicely, the sweet smoke blooming out of chimneys. Miceal and his tin whistle mourned the death of the day.

– Someone saw ye with the tinker.

That, as we came near our house.

– Who?

– It does not matter.

– What does not matter? Who saw me, or the fact that I drank with a tinker?

– I do not know.

And his eyes looked confused, his shoulders hunched to guard himself.

– Sean, why does everyone dislike the tinkers? They've made me tea, have treated me with civility, and today Christy King bought me a drink. These are things any of the islanders would do for a stranger.

– Aye, but ye cannot trust a tinker.

– What have they ever done to you?

– It is not what they have done to meself, it is what ye hear: that they steal cattle, milk the cows of honest men on the sly, make friendly with the wives of others, camp where they are not wanted. They are always moving on so they do not take the blame for their sins.

– Don't you think God punishes the wicked, whether they have a cottage or a caravan? You always talk about

His justice. Do you not think the tinkers are under His eyes?

He did not know how to reply. Then: Ye always take the side of the others, the fish or the tinkers. Ye are always wanting to leave the sharks alone when they come to tear our nets, and where would we get the money for another? And ye will defend a tinker who is known in these parts for his crafty ways. Have ye not allegiance with the honest folk?

– What do you think?

– I do not know any more.

– Well, until I came to Inishbream, I was very like the tinkers, wasn't I?

☦ ☦ ☦

– Brigid of the miracles, I cannot compete with the wind in a wild man's heart, and I ask to be forgiven, to be allowed to cast my lot to the stone soul of this island.

– Child, I will teach you the sign of the blessing, the sign of all devotion.

Sean visited the crone, telling of a distance. She said, Take the stone which the English call lodestone. You will know it by its sad blue colour. Lay this stone under the head of thy wife, and if she be chaste, she will embrace her husband.

I did not see the tinkers leave, uprooting the bright blossoming of their residence and leaving the hills barren as before their coming.

Sometimes I dream of a garden behind a broken hedge, I dream of caravans, all the beauty of the long road before them.

And I did embrace.

A Gale from the West

DEATH COMES ON A GALE from the west, sly at first, then pummelling down on the house of the ailing. Or, unloosed at sea, turns currachs mouthdown in the water, and the fishermen sink with their emptied lungs.

– Can you swim?
– We cannot. If the sea wants ye, she will have ye, and it is better to go easy so.

The cemetery is locked against casual entry, walled in stone and gated with a rusted bed frame, four great boulders preventing its fall to an interested cow or God knows what. Crosses, watermarked and sprouting an assortment of lichens, indicate the ancestors, the mounds themselves indistinguishable under cowslips or sea thrift.

– When was the last burial?
– Wasn't it only last year when the child of Mairtin died of the fever. That'll be the little cross ye may see there (pointing). And the drowned three of four years back, and I think meself that the fourth one who never washed up ought to be given a cross, too. Didn't we keen for him, same as the other lads, and didn't we board up his

house? Ah, tis a shame and that's the truth that he was never given a deal box and put to earth.

– And no one ever found anything of him?

– Not even his jumper or least one Wellington, and didn't yer man on the Arans write a play that said, as we say, that you can tell who a drowned man is by the pattern of his woman on the gansey, and wouldn't we know if he ever washed up? There are the telephones now. Ye cannot keep things quiet in this ould county. And there are suicides of which ye must not talk. They are buried where the two boreens cross; tis the place of no arrival.

Death comes on a gale from the west, leaving a carnage of birds, seals, the trapped fish in the loosened nets.

– What do you suppose that mound is (pointing out the door to a swelling of earth behind the house)?

– Tis the midden from the other days.

– The midden?

– Aye, where they tossed the leavings of the kitchen, the broken crocks and whatever else.

– Do you mean your parents?

– I do not. They burned and buried their refuse, same as we do. I mean the original islanders, the oldest ones, older even than the crone or Miceal the elder, the ones Cromwell drove to Connacht so many years ago.

I don't think the midden looks any different than the grave mounds. They have their bleak, composed stones; the midden has an empty whiskey bottle; but the length and bulk are nearly identical. I say nothing and wait for a good moon.

Candles. A small trowel. The dog and my man bedded down for the sleeping. A nightjar calls from Inishturk, is answered. I begin to scrape away soil from the side of the midden. The trowel clangs softly on the edge of a discovery. Bones, I think — the sound very like enamel. I dig down. I imagine the earth enriched by marrow and flesh; I imagine the beauty of ribs against dark loam. And I unearth a piece of pottery, in no way vertebral but chunky and solid, wonderfully soft, the glaze dulled and shattered by the years and smelling of earthworms.

I want to go deeper into the midden. I want to discover a whole elaborate system of worship, the bodies prepared for transition, food alongside, fossilized and ancient in aspect, bowls, weapons.

I find the black and hardened peels of potatoes cast to the heap a century before and protected by the bog-earth; I find little dried cabbage stalks, pared to the quick, and a bowl, a mortar, cracked in half.

I want to discover the secrets of the island, the unchristened children of the wayward daughters, the epileptic dogs. A grandmother.

✠ ✠ ✠

– Would you mind if I went to visit Shelagh?
– For how long would ye be gone?
– A week. I'd like to go for a week.
– Aye. Of course I can manage. Go to her so and enjoy yerself.

So I went with the post that Tuesday and drove up as far as Westport with the Electricity Supply Board man.

– Thirteen moons last year, and what's it to bring us, I ask ye? The last time we saw such a thing was the year preceding the Great Famine.

– Oh.

The rocks of Leenane Harbour were thick with mussels, and all along the south Mayo road there were sheep clustered close to the crumbling shoulders. On the brink of Croagh Patrick we passed a tinker camp. I knew no one but waved to the curious children, the inevitable dogs.

– This is where I must be dropping ye.

– Thanks for the lift. Have a good day.

– And yerself, God willing.

I took up my rucksack and strode through the narrow streets of Westport, watched by shapes from every window. The clock in the square spoke its constancy. A few cats darted about the shop displays. When I reached the Castlebar road, it was my luck that a car stopped almost immediately.

– I will be going as far as Ballina.

– Oh good. Will you drop me at Turlough?

– I will indeed. But why, may I ask, would ye ever be wanting Turlough?

– My friend lives there.

– In Turlough? And has she always lived so?

– No. She was married to a Turlough man. He died, and she went away, and now she's come back.

– Ah, would she ever be the ould lady in the caravan?
– How do you know?
– Ye cannot keep things quiet in this county.

We drove along. The land changed as we left the sea coast, air dulling and losing its iodine sting, land acquiring trees and shrubs from the slow, ripe atmosphere. Signs, pointing firmly down side roads, suggested grand towns, though I knew I'd find only a single pub selling bread, chocolate and wrinkled apples as well as the spirits, and there would be a house or two planted alongside. Villages I knew I'd never know, pubs I knew I'd never drink in, and the stories, Oh most of all the stories I'd never hear: the Civil War hero who had single-handedly chased the English back where they came from, and God they'd stay finally with their language and their religion (*Church of England, do ye mind, and not believing in the Pope!*); Pats Maloney, master of poteen distillation, and there was a day he tricked the Garda; Breda Ryan with the best legs in all the counties, and didn't yer fine Dublin man say so, and didn't he buy her the roses which sat on the bar in Cready's pub to prove it to all who'd see them? I sat in the tragedy of a road leading directly and never thinking to meander back into the hills beyond the bog or stopping in a momentary way to take the sun with a hamlet's oldest farmer.

The driver broke into my thoughts. Will ye have a pint in Castlebar?

– Yes, I'd like that.

We stopped in the dark, smallish public house, greeted

by the red sign with its single glass of Guinness dead centre. There was the usual assortment of homey men: mended jackets, shaggy caps, gapped teeth and the startling eyes of a true lover.

– Ah, ye pour a good pint of stout, Michael Joe.

There was a way of drinking the pint. You cradled the glass a moment in your hands, your fingers stroking the curves and the wetness; you sniffed the creamy top, pressing your mouth ever so softly on the rim, just to have a suggestion of what you'd be knowing as the pint really settled. Then you'd lick your mouth and you'd be delighted. And the pint would be excellent. You'd never doubt that.

> *As I roved out on a bright May morning,*
> *To view the flowers and meadows gay . . .*

Someone's noble voice singing there at the bar, and the others listening in an honest respect.

> *If I married the lassie that had the land, my love,*
> *It's that I'll rue until the day I die . . .*

Then we were on the road to Ballina, we were exclaiming at the rich green of the hayfields and the contented munching cattle, and then it was Turlough: two pubs, Mrs. Loughran's and her mother's; Delia's store; and a row of houses, the one at the end crumbling to the day.

The man hummed. *I am a wee weaver . . .* Then: Yer sure ye won't come on to Ballina, just for the crack?

A pickup if I ever saw one. No. Shelagh's waiting.

She was there in the caravan up from Loughran's pub in the shadow of the round tower, there in the sunny window, waving. Her cats scattered.

– Ah, you're looking well. I've made scones and have the tea ready. You're welcome here. Take off the rucksack and come in!

The caravan was an enchanted place of Moroccan baskets, Wicklow weaving, a pie of Saint George's mushrooms gathered in the cool Charlebois wood, sorrel, wild garlic keeping cool in a glass, one wall of books (Krishnamurti, *Culpeper's Herbal*, the works of all the visionaries), candles in brass pots.

✢ ✢ ✢

– What happened to the roof?

We were walking in the Charlebois wood and happened upon a splendid view of the old house, the hunting lodge, where Shelagh and her husband had lived in the long ago. The house, elegant though roofless, ancestral under the wry sun.

– Ah, there was such a wind and it took the roof and didn't it just land in a field fourteen miles away, shaking the farmer out of a year's growth. That was just after Gerald died and myself not a true Fitzwarren (only by marriage), and so I took up a few wee things and went to live in Tunisia. For the arthritis, bad even then.

– Oh.

And she continued through the forest, small and graceful in her age, pausing to touch the moss of the trees her son Edward had planted in the peaceful summers before his lover drove him mad. I remained at the edge of the view. Took off my shoes. Clenched in my toes the soft grass, earth, leaves, a startled purple-backed beetle. The rare sun entered the chapel of trees through the vaulted branches. Leaned my back on a stump, my spine fitting nicely into the pungent wood. Warm. Breathless. Thought: You could stay here always. Forget the stones of Inishbream, the obsessive stories of drowning. You have always loved trees, and it is the custom in this county to offer your lover a dowry grove, planted by your father or someone as generous. Thought: You'd never be found if you built your shelter in this forest she has declared a sanctuary for birds, foxes of the hills, badgers, anything wild and fond of burrows.

– And are you coming on, then? I've the tea laid out.

I walked upright out of the forest, and we drank tea on the porch of the breezy house, ate apples and biscuits.

– Did you like the old wood, then? I always think of it as Edward's wood. He loved it so. I wanted to bury him here, but I hadn't the money to bring his body back from London.

Thought: How lovely to be buried in the Charlebois earth, the ground soft with heron feathers, the night hollow with the chanting hooves. Not hard sea and that drumming rain.

I came away incoherent with her stories. The brother in Russia. (It was so odd in London to be handing out the anti-war pamphlets on Hyde Park Corner and to see him with his communist tracts on the opposite side, and when our father died and himself the eldest, didn't he sign over the fortune and the home to the Dublin trade-unions?) The mother, an astrologer in the wilds of Dunkineely, and I'd spent whole mornings in a book of the planets she'd left to Shelagh, smelling of age and brittle fingers and annotated in the margins with a faint spidery pencil. The brother in South Africa. (The young woman he lives with a widow, her husband having strangled himself with a nylon stocking in one of his queer perversions. Bind himself to the bed, he would, and then play with himself. Can you believe such a thing?) The son and the daughter, both gifted and both suicides, photographs of them as children, the full sensual lips of Edward. Years later, his arm on the tweed chest of his lover, in a suit, the casual scarf at his neck. The stories of the early Charlebois: hunters all with their feet by the fire cleaning their guns, the maids, the meals of venison and jugged hare, and good potatoes splitting their sides, all floury. And then the travelling, after her husband's death by water, long stays in Spain, Tunisia, the Channel Islands out of season. And the immediate dream of a cottage in Donegal, her birthplace, and the bracing air her blood still longed to.

I came away stirred and a little mad for her past myself,

her filled and tangled years. I would be the archaeologist of her old age, carefully brushing the dust off the artifacts as they unearthed themselves from a living ground. A book, the only one of Edward's she kept; a piece of mountain pottery from Spain.

It was a long route home, first through the sultry air, sky thick with the fattened Mayo birds, then to the coast road, the rain and clutter of small boats populating the fjord of Leenane.

When I arrived in Clifden, it was to discover that half the island population had come over to shop, taking advantage of a high enough tide to be able to go right into Clifden Bay in the currachs.

You could tell the islanders from the townspeople easily enough, though the differences seem nearly nonexistent in the telling. Well, it's the way they dress, warmly, and the women are always carrying several loaded bags, are never without a head scarf. Or their accents are broader, they use odd expressions. But an islander would tell you the accents differ from farm to farm on the mainland and from rock to rock off it. And on a rainy day, not a soul would be found barehaded on earth. Perhaps I mean that it was the atmosphere they moved in that made them different. And the way the men made their effortless perfect knots when they tied the boats at the town quay, the way their respect for the sea brightened their very flesh and eyes, the way even their skeletons seemed an almanac of the world they knew in a language difficult in the learning but natural to the born initiate. The careful movement of feet on town cobbles, as though they were walking over algae-slick shore stone or in the belly of a pukaun, bracing themselves for the bringing in of nets.

– Ah, so yer back. And had ye a good small holiday?

– Yes, Peter. But Mayo is so different, isn't it? Even the air.

– Aye, tis so, but it seems we have not lost ye to it. Now. Sean has not come to the town this day and so ye may go back with meself, but first I will be proceeding to Eamon's for a bit of a drink. Will ye join me?

– I will.

We took our whiskey neat in the smoky, familiar dark. The drunken woman from Ballyconneely was singing at the bar:

If you are going across the water,
Take me with you to be your partner . . .

– Ah, Peggy, yerra girl. Eamon, would ye ever give the lady another vodka?

How could she have known "Donal Og" was his favourite song, and why did she sing so directly to him?

– Thank ye, Peter.

Then more of "Donal Og": *I'll do your milking and nurse your baby . . .*

Peter hastily declared himself at odds with the malt, and we began to make our slow descent to the currach. We were riding the current home to Inishbream, the air stinging and a music to our ears.

What greeted me upon the event of my return: the children of Mairtin; the elderly dog, dusty and soft in the tooth; the calves, anxious to take my fingers in their mouths for the familiar feeling of a mother if not the taste; the wind rasping through the elephant grass about the stark, cliff-hanging cottage of my marriage; and my man, a startling tangle of sun-bleached hair and arms full of nets, which were dropped. And the arms filled with myself.

One of the old men died, the eldest man in the house of brothers. They had been expecting it for years but finding him cold and blue in the bed was a shock. Overnight. No one heard a sound from him, although they all slept in the same room. One brother said, Sure and how can ye expect to hear anything, even yer own heart, when the gales blow and beat on the doors, shaking every pane of the windows.

What I knew of him: that he was simple, that he walked with two sticks, and sometimes I'd see him at the far end of the island, bent in the wind like a thorn tree. I knew that as a young man he'd gone to America and had come back for his father's funeral, never to leave again. Some said he wanted to marry Kathleen long ago, before she was bearded, and her refusal was his reason for leaving in the first place.

There was the all-night vigil by the body, the watchers

fortified by poteen, and then the priest came, and the boulders were rolled away from the gate of the cemetery. The mourners entered and stood in the rain as the priest invoked God and angels, and then the coffin was lowered into the grave men had carved out of the difficult earth. Covered it. A few heart-shaped boxes of artificial roses, wrapped in plastic, lay upon the mound, the ink of the sympathy cards running thin. There was a hymn and prayer. The crone was audibly hoarse from the keening she'd performed during the long wake. The brothers were grim-faced and silent.

A gale from the west, pummelling down on the house of the ailing.

SEA AREA FORECAST

IT WILL SEEM, IN THIS TELLING, that my days followed one upon the other actively, like flights of geese or shoals of breeding mackerel. Never tiresome or moth-eaten. And there *were* moths, soft-winged buggers that made a quick lacy work of shirts and a favourite woollen shawl.

Yet I remember whole weeks of lethargy, whole compositions of boredom when I dreamed of going to Paris. Street theatre, the white-faced mimes, jugglers, dark coffee in the Deux Magots. I dreamed of Greece and the night-dancing, the supple men and their unbearable swaying pelvises. Letters arrived from friends: "We are going to Portugal (you'd like the fish-cobbled streets), to Afghanistan. Oh, we'd love to have you with us." I wrote back: "I fish. My bread goes pale blue with mould because I have no fridge or damp-free box."

There was a man who went away, and often I dreamed of following, of hunting the roadside camps for a blue-eyed devil. There were meals of potatoes and anaemic cabbages, washed out and sour. Trips to town, a nineteenth-century opus of two streets and fifteen pubs. Nights illuminated by a cool moon, the shy crackle of a candle's flame.

Then the butcher offered me a young mare to break and train as my own.

— She's a flighty filly, pure Connemara, but too small for me, so ye could manage her, I'm thinking. Come and see her. If ye like her, she's yers so.

She was grey as smoke and fourteen hands, a fine Araby head, and long-legged. Her nostrils against my palm were the softest on earth as I fed her a scrawny carrot. Warm, too, and her flanks rippled as I ran my hand across her back.

— Rising three, she is, and ready for the saddle.

But there was a problem: how to get her to the island and where to ride her once she got there. She could swim, of course. I remembered the Sable Island ponies swimming a far greater distance. But no man could touch them, and they ran for centuries in their wrath and solitude for such an abandonment. And this mare would arrive furious and terrified and would never trust the mistress who led her there. Once on the island, there was not one level area fit for the schooling of a green horse. The cows trod the rocks on their cloven hooves. One mile by one mile. I knew the mare would splinter her hooves on the flinty lane.

— No, Malachy, I guess I'd better not have her.

My calves were growing too large to keep by the house; you could not open a door without them barging headlong into the kitchen, upsetting the churn and the teacups.

— I'll move 'em so to the far field.

They showed the whites of their eyes as they left. Horseless, childless and now without cattle, I was a sorry excuse for an islandwoman.

The colour of those weeks was grey. Grey as far as you

could see or feel. I remembered a joke I'd heard in Canada: Baffin Island wanted its independence from the provinces and territories, and its flag would be a polar bear standing against a snowdrift. White on white. I bought a colour box to make paintings of Inishbream. I kept mixing black with white to make grey. Never used the crimson or the aquamarine. Never used purple or the spring green. Grey on grey. Those were my paintings.

The bright moments do not sound bright in a truthful accounting. The sea thrift, when picked, lost its shell-pink flowers, and you could not expect a jug of them to last more than an afternoon. But they had their quick splendour, gracing the table in a handleless blue-willow cup. And if I lay stomach-down in the meadow by my house, I could see a brilliance of wild cowslips that lost their sun underneath the tall dullish grass. Oh, and I tell you, there were brief, shuddering, brilliant marriages under the quilt, accompanied by the static poem of the night.

> *Here is the sea area forecast. Meteorological situation at 21 hours: a moist westerly airflow covers Ireland. A frontal trough lies over the north of the country . . .*

And the husband's stuttering hands.

> *. . . all Irish coastal waters and Irish sea. Wind: west or southwest force 3 or 4, backing southwest to south force 3 to 5 tomorrow.*

There was the intimacy of the announcer's voice in the dark room, recognizing the correspondence of bodies fronting and backing and the holiness of fingers laced or woven into hair.

Visibility: 1 to 3 miles in rain or drizzle. Less than 400 yards in fog. Otherwise over 10 miles. Further outlook . . .

The part I waited for like an oracle's prediction.

. . . light to moderate south or southwest winds. Occasional rain showers, especially in the west.

And then there was the chant of reports from coastal stations, the litany for boats and men.

Malin Head: southwest, 10 kts, drizzle, 6 mls, 1016 mbs, rising slowly. Valentia: south, 10 kts, cloudy, 11 mls, 1018 mbs, steady. Belmullet: south, 9 kts, recent drizzle, 11 mls, 1016 mbs, steady.

Yes, especially in the west, Valentia, Belmullet, our own Slyne Head. You could look on any atlas precipitation chart, and according to the legend, the fraction of paper that was the Connemara coast would be the wettest in all Ireland. The chart colour for rainfall was green. And I remembered the first day greening on the island of my home, the deep growth of salal and bright-berried kinnikinnick, the ferns. The patron saint of all life was greenfingered, the rising sea wrack shot with green light, and I saw the rabbits of Eyrephort stricken with myxomatosis that summer, dying a green young death.

Remembering Winter

I REMEMBER FIELDS OF STONE and a harrowing, men dragging chains behind them, a burden on their backs. Earth separated itself from stones, silting through the links, finally furrowing on the slight rise of the garden.

– If ye can, just toss them big ladeens off to the side, then we can trowel the rest of 'em under so.

And there were buckets of musty seed potatoes, eyes sprouting in darkness, there were fleshy cabbages, and little else to go into the ground. Maybe the occasional row of carrots that would emerge from the loam when pulled fiercely by their tops, and they'd be burrowy with worms and woody to the taste. Parsnips, two-forked and convoluted like ancient fertility charms. Or else parsley to brighten the first pan of new potatoes, then left to dry in any sun that might occur.

In another area, lovely grainy rye for thatch, for fodder, for the secret stills of the island evenings.

I remember the rains of summer and the green shoots. After the harvest there was nothing. Dark earth and the shorn fields. The fatted calf hanging skinless from a beam.

— We will be given the Council houses next summer. That is the promise.

— How do you know?

— Some of the others, Festy and Peter, have been inquiring. They have told of the fierce cold, the old with their rheumatism, the shortage of turf and the drowning. This is not a new promise. They have been telling us we'll have the houses all right, but they are not so quick with the making of them.

The new houses, held in the future like a bright flower to make the coming winter bearable. I walked the various roads where the allocated ground held the foundations, saw the design in the one finished bungalow: square, white, and the trim a bright yellow; a barren, treeless yard; no more a part of the landscape than the power boats of the summer people seemed a part of the sea. Transplants, grafts, utterly unnatural.

— Will you be glad to move?

— Ah, when ye have spent a winter here, ye will not ask such a question.

The lanes seemed strangely empty when I walked them. The small shy children were now confined to the schoolhouse, though still barefooted and with sun-bleached hair. And the currachs were in, black beetles in the fall days, shiny with new tar and patchy with the mending. The pots were anchored with rocks along the quay top or else were stacked in various sculleries to be restrung. Tangly nets, filling the outbuildings, reeked of fish guts and were littered with the broken legs of crabs and the dried scales of mackerel.

✼ ✼ ✼

You will not say you were lonely. If it was conversation you wanted, then it could be found on the lane by the quay any evening. You could find your way to it by the thin smoke rising from the pipes, even in rain; you could follow the low music of voices. Or, in the kitchen of the house that was the post office (stamps in a tin box, letters bound with string), the women would be at the knitting, pausing now and then to reprimand a child. And there was the man in the narrow marriage bed, the smell of salt in his hair. In a purely simple way, you could say you were happy with your tasks.

But then you'd walk and could only pace the single mile of island ground before retracing your steps or stopping in the face of the sea. You'd wait for a change in the shape of the land, a seasonal turning of tides. They'd turn and change quickly, unnoticed out the window. Spring tide, neap tide, a minimal wearing of stone under the force of the elements: mostly rain. At harvest, you'd expected riches, not the perfunctory pulling of onions from the unrewarding earth.

What you did not expect: winter. You did not expect the terrible frosts and the sly damp that filled every inch of the cottage and found its way into your bones, making the old fractures of wrist and pelvis ache under the layers of clothing you had naively believed to be a protection. Your bed was clammy and smelled of mildew. There was no fishing. The days you spent listening to weather reports on the wireless, hoping for a reprieve and drinking tea from a pot you would not allow to be empty. Or else you tried to untangle the cat's cradle your knitting had become, your numb fingers twisting at the knots and counting the stitches, only to discover the knots were permanent and most of the stitches had fallen. You tried to read the library books you'd choose on the one day in a fortnight that boats would venture to the mainland, and you wept at the descriptions of an island the October ferry was sailing to, the driftwood of its shores bleached and huge as dinosaur bones, an island which you knew well. The newspapers promised nothing but cutbacks and strikes and colder temperatures than had ever been known. You made soup. What else could you do? But you could barely stand to use potatoes that had begun to sprout or carrots that had gone tasteless in their box. And the redeeming summer nettles had been trimmed to the roots or else were rotten with rain. So everything you made was flavoured strongly with onions and the secrecy of herbs you kept in a dark cupboard, reminding you of an earlier island where you had lived on a hill of wild rosemary and sage, their blossoms bright and pungent even in the depths of December. And there was never enough turf to make a really hot fire, and you had to ration it, never knowing from one day to the next whether you could go to the mainland for another load.

You wondered about the tinker, imagined him in the swarthy light of a winter caravan, maybe playing a tin whistle to the melancholy night. The man you thought you knew became more silent in winter, and he joined the other men in a kitchen you were not invited to, nor were any other women. You knew they warmed themselves with poteen. You could smell it when he returned. But what they talked of, or knew in their collective silence, God kept to Himself.

You despaired at the sight of the other women knitting their jerseys and mittens and caps, unfolding them like magic from the chanting needles. You did not have a child to scold or to wrap in your arms. The elderly dog slept. The calves, moved to a far field, grown large and red-eyed (and one dead), munched the mouldy hay you trundled to them and no longer welcomed your fingers.

You sat damply in a chair pulled as close to the tiny mound of smouldery turf as you dared, you thought of the rest of the winters of your life spent like this in the bitter cold, your fingers arthritic before their time and your nose sniffly, and you knew you could not bear it.

I gave my own names to things that winter. The seals had all fled Carrickarona, and there were only ever a few scraggy seabirds who happened to land on their way somewhere else: *I name thee the Rocks of Desolation.*

Or the cliffs of Ardmore, with their echoes of a house

I had known in a milder winter on Vancouver Island, now stony-faced, no gentle covering of heather or pale thrift: *I name thee the Cliffs of Peril.*

And the man whom I had taken as a lover, as a husband: *I name thee Stranger.*

They were long months made longer by the refusal of spring. Festy's cow, deceived by one warmish day, calved on the next, and when they found the calf, it was opaque with frost and quite dead. The children shed coats that same day and were bronchial for months.

– This is likely to be the last winter we shall spend here. The new houses are promised us so.

I said nothing. Christmas, too, had been a promise, and when it came I was lonely for another family; their phone call did not bridge the continents but widened all oceans unspeakably. It did not help that Sean got drunk as a lord and had to be walked in the wind to sober him. (Christmas. I had thought of presents, naturally, and wreaths on doors and trees blooming in the corners of kitchens, bright with candles and tinsel. I imagined sweetmeats and shortbread, plum pudding and wassail. But no. Where would a tree come from? Finland? Or heaven? There was a horrible lardy cake, and we ate a scrawny chicken from the brothers' flock. And we ate potatoes. Someone brought poteen. That was Sean's present. I had nothing.)

If Saint Paul's Day be fair and clear,
It does betide a happy year.

If clouds or mist do dark the sky,
Great stores of birds and beasts shall die.

And January twenty-fifth, the feast of Saint Paul, was a grim day, dark as night, mottled with mist and followed by a series of identical twins.

Agnes O'Keefe had a baby that March, a blasted crier of all hours and terrible with wrinkles. Her husband, father of at least five that he'd claim, was proud and used the birth as occasion for what was probably the worst drunk of his life. Or the best, depending on your perspective. Mine, from the scullery window, saw him up to his knees in the wintry sea, singing "The Mountain Streams Where the Moorcocks Crow" in a monotone. And this, three days after. A kind of baptism, a kind of impossible joy, for I knew the child would not be special or gifted with a talent for much. There was too much inbreeding in the O'Keefe family, and the children all had the heavy brows of the simple. They drooled. I don't remember if the new baby was a girl or a boy.

The point is, despite my notations of stone works and thin soil, the island possessed its own queer fecundity, and not only in March. Children were born with an astonishing regularity, which meant that the winters were not completely fruitless and without warmth under the damp bedclothes. People bred, animals bred. There was a rhythm, instinctive for life, that must have resounded deep in the body of the island. And I did not often hear it.

In April I caught a fever of purification, and I mixed lime and water, passing a brush over the dull lichens and the sooty fireplace wall. I painted the window sashes brilliant green and bought geraniums on a trip to town to brighten the stone wall and cover the bird shit. Then, done with it all, I crouched near the fire; the frosts recognized no calendar or polite seasonal order, and I'd been mittenless all through the painting. The next week, I cursed myself for not bringing the geraniums in overnight because they were brown and limp in the morning air, crisp with frost, and I threw them as far as I could to the sea. The first wind claimed its share of whitewash, leaving the cottage bruised under its fine assault.

All the oratories were in ruin, the chapels of stone falling, and the communities drawn together by love of God and need of man were breaking apart and scattering. We are always sailing to islands, lured by the thought of sleeping above the waters of birth and death. And we may be born on islands, forever drawn back to them all our lives just as the white horses of waves are drawn to the shore, and we will be broken when we arrive.

If I'd been Brendan, I'd never have stopped for long on the Island of Sheep and the Island of Birds, I'd never have drifted, I'd have sailed right on until I arrived on the coast of Newfoundland. And if I'd been with the fishermen of Inishbream who'd greeted his successor, I'd have begged on my knees in the bottom of the currach, I'd have begged to be taken along.

✠ ✠ ✠

It is written that when the grey geese fly over the promised grave of a man, he will shiver. During that winter on Inishbream, the world's entire population of geese, all colours, moved in constant untiring circles over my grave.

Yet milder weather finally came. Not quickly or with a tremendous rising of the temperatures, so that you'd forget in a moment all the hours of ice and the beginnings of chilblains. No. But there'd be a day when all the layers seemed too many, and you'd remove one accordingly. Never the oilskin; you were never trusting enough for that, but maybe one jersey. Then another day, another layer, and so on. And there you were, a simple shirt and trousers and pale sun fine on your face and maybe your toes if you'd gone that far.

The seals returned to Carrickarona, an alchemy of air, water and grey rock creating them in such great numbers that the twilight was filled with their barking. The island cows began to drop their calves one by one in the lengthening days, and their milk was rich with the abundance of clover and buttercups they'd been feeding on.

The mended nets and pots were ready for any goers. The weather was still too cool to be worth the trying for lobsters, but on a windy night you could put out nets and be sure of a few fat salmon. It was good to be on the water. I'd forgotten the way the seabirds called the morning alive like a craggy hymn, I'd forgotten the beauty of green mesh shoaling through the water as the nets were lowered and the stone weights led them far below.

The island was a softer home now that the flowers were out and the business of fishing was underway. The calves capered on their stilty legs behind the crumbling walls and the cows were proud in their aspect, all but Festy's cow with her terrible loss, the calf in its bag of blue membrane left coldly for the dogs.

PATTERNS OF EVOLUTION

LISTEN. I *want* to say that everything was all right in the spring, that the brown geraniums floated in on the tide, miraculously blooming, that the bruised cottage healed white in the sun. I want to tell you that the drowned man washed up, maybe as a changeling or a merman but himself inside.

But miracles happen in their own way, are not willed or dreamed in the hard hours. They come out of the sky or the heart, unexpected and awesome as the will of God.

The truth is, I'd have left with the tinker if I thought it would help, desire the halter and a setting free. I'd have migrated with the geese if I'd had the supple wings. Now I wanted to leave alone, forever and completely.

Everyone was excited about the new houses. *Running water, indoor toilets! Can ye imagine . . . And we'll not be cut off in the winter, we can shop whenever we fancy . . .*

— Well, yer man in charge promises them for September.

— Ah, then the children can start the year in the town school so.

They imagined a future behind an elegance of sheer curtains (*from Galway, mind ye, and three quid a pair!*), each window identical, and inside, hot water, not the blessed nuisance of running to the well and heating kettles for the washing. There'd be clotheslines, too, and there'd not be the bother of drying on the stone walls, sleeves and hems anchored by island granite. The children would learn their lessons as was proper, inside, and they'd not be at the whim of a first-year trainee who would lead them down the lane to the tidal pools or along the dunes to identify each bloom, the Gaelic names falling from their tongues like water.

I worried about the old men, the ones who never left the island, not even for the cattle fair. I wondered how the future would treat them when they were settled into the bungalows miles from each other and a couple in plain view of Inishbream. I wanted to believe that they'd be lonely off the rock they'd been born on and rooted to over the centuries in a long hereditary way. I hoped they'd find the loss too unbearable to live with, that they'd return unceremoniously, perhaps in the night, rowing home over the mussel-black sea. But probably they'd survive and would grow even older without the distorting knots to their joints that the island arthritis bequeathed them.

And I will say, although I wanted to leave sometimes so badly my throat ached and my heart tugged at its contrary tethers, I did want the islanders to remain, selfish as it may be. I wanted to know that somewhere a place existed outside the rhythm of life as we know it, peculiar to its geography, dependent on weather and moving in time to an unheard bodrhan. I read books about islands, needing to clarify or confirm my belief in the holiness of isolated land:

> *The patterns of evolution on islands usually dictate that insular organisms be overtaken. A strong atmosphere of vulnerability broods over them. The fact that island beings are not weedy, do not predominate, and are not in the grist of commerce and domestication does not mean that they are mere curiosities. They are part of the entire pattern of life on earth, and without them, the entire pattern would be incomplete, even meaningless.*

Yes, I said, yes. And I was afraid.

That summer had a temporary holiday feeling to it. There was no need to make fodder for the coming winter out of sparse dry grass, scything it down, raking it, pulling net over the mounds finally in deference to the wind and planting a ring of stones around each to hold it. It was likely most of the cattle would be sold in the summer sales because the Council plots were too small to provide much graze. The school was not whitewashed, the family sequence of duty broken that once, then forever. And the turf was brought over in small quantities, most of it waiting on the bog to be brought to the new houses.

One night on the wireless there was a documentary about an island to the south that was slowly losing its inhabitants to the mainland. One or two families were left. They were interviewed, the announcer asking questions about island life, individual histories, and in the silences between words, the sound was of wind incanting, terns mewing, breaking waves on the rocky perimeter.

– I'd say their plight was very like ours now. Did ye hear yer man telling about the turf shortages and the terrible problems they had getting a doctor for the sick, a priest for the dying, so that they may go to earth settled, like?

– Aye, and trying to grow yer potatoes in a soil God cursed from the beginning.

I remembered lonely birds in a gale, knew inside the brutality of wind when you were at its horrid, belligerent mercy, but I thought how silent life on any earth would be without its constant punctuation of the day.

– Have ye a story this night that ye can tell to pass the hours?

– I haven't. You tell one.

– Well, now. All I can think for the telling is yer man in Mweenish who trains the sheepdogs, and didn't a Mayo man arrange to buy one. So he collects the beast and brings it home, I don't know, to Achill or Newport. That evening, he takes it out to bring in the sheep. Here's the dog, looking at the man like he's an eejit, waiting for orders, and yer man is telling the beast over and over what he wants him to do. The dog, he thinks, is deaf. So he takes him all the way back to Mweenish and tells the breeder. And do ye know what was wrong?

— No, what?

— The dog knew only the Irish, coming from Mweenish like, and yer man was giving out to him in English.

— Couldn't the man speak Irish then?

— Not a word, or maybe just one. But there. Someone else got the dog who could speak Irish and would, and the Mayo lad got another beast trained to the English.

But what if he liked the dog, I thought to myself.

There were always stories. I liked to hear about the time the lads climbed the cliffs of High Island to shoot a Christmas goose, though it wasn't *my* year. Or about Joe Mulloy on Inishturk, whose hands were so large they spanned the width of an accordion. Or the building of the film star's house above Eyrephort, out of rock, and himself bringing beer to the workers. I liked to think of Stephen Clancy painting the navigational Mother of Jesus each spring so she'd stand out for the safety of all sailors. *Mother of Christ, star of the sea, pray for the wanderer, pray for me.* And there were tales of the children now departed, their letters shared in the evenings and their occasional visits, from London or Boston or even Dublin, anticipated for months. Years, some of them.

I liked the story about the seal who came up in the trammel net, dead of course, but his feasting mouth still full of the brilliant back of a salmon. Of the swans on Omey Strand who'd walk the sand like holidaymakers.

And then the same strand under the harvest moon, shadowed by the twisting embrace of the silverfish diggers, and then a smell all over Connemara of the frying catch. Then there were the ghosts seen by one at a time and sworn to in the names of the Father and Son (the moaning of the drowned man down by the shore). There were the wakes and the weddings, made spectacular by poteen.

The crone remembered the days when the turf was known all over the west for the fine burning you could expect of it. *Those hookers would come in to the quay from Galway or Barna, and they'd load the turf in. Ye could never cut and foot enough, they'd be wanting so much. Now yer lucky to find an ould scraw wedged there where once was the finest bog ever. Ah, tis a pity and a sorrow to ourselves that we cannot provide our own turf any longer.*

There'd be a story at any hour when you could locate two or more people together and at leisure, on the boreen, in a kitchen or enjoying a comfortable pipe after the last net had been untangled and laid to rest over the wall. My favourite time of the day was twilight, when Miceal would play his tin whistle to the stones and the sea and whoever would listen.

– Would you please play the Breton piece?
– Aye.

It seemed that even the stupid blind wind would subside when Miceal's bent fingers jigged over the length of the whistle, and instead of its hollow, monotonous tones there'd be the sweet, sad airs of the Celtic heart.

Someone else wanted reels or "The Raggle Taggle

Gypsies." We listened till the cows came home. When it darkened, you could see the frail lights begin to bloom on Bream and Turk and the occasional headlamps of evening cars on the Sky Road. The summer people would drive to the mainland viewpoint and would park, casting their beams over Mannin Bay and out to the islands. They'd see the pale gaslight or candlelight smudging the dark of the archipelago and the long piercing flash of Slyne Head, the keepers over each season attentive to craft warnings and the forecasting of gales. And if they stepped out of their cars, they'd hear the mourning donkeys and the last notes of "The Woman of the House."

The islanders said they'd never known a wetter summer, and wet it was, the sun only showing its face once in a blue moon and a weak sun at that, waterlogged in an earthbound sky.

It rained for days at a time. The nettles flourished. The roof leaked in a place or two, and you could not sleep some nights for the steady drumming of rain on the slates, then the water ringing into tin pans underneath. It was a seven days' wonder that the turf burned at all.

When it didn't rain, there was mist, grey and soft on your face and so thick you would swear if need be that there was no mainland at all, only the edges of the island and the image of your own hand in front of your face.

✠ ✠ ✠

A strange bird on the byre one morning. I asked, What kind of bird is that?

— Oh, save us! This is a bad sign. Did ye never hear the rhyme . . . I don't know, is it Irish? . . . one magpie sorrow, two stand for joy . . . well, we can be taking it to mean that someone will die within the year.

— Yes, we have that verse, but we say "crow." I've never seen a magpie before. He's a big bird.

— Sure and wicked as sin. Only last year Paddy Bourke saw one of them ladeens on his roof and a month later didn't his brother Tom at Aillebrack die.

— Do you believe it?

— Oh, you must. Because it happens, you see.

The magpie stayed several hours on the roof of the byre, grooming himself and looking about curiously. Without the white, I'd have thought him a rook. He hunched further into his feathers, blinked. It was odd the way the morning seemed empty of other birds: fulmars, petrels, and especially the starlings whose shadows would haunt the garden for seeds, the porch for crumbs, and even a bold one coming into the scullery, bumping into windows until it stunned itself and I removed the quivery body to the outside sill. I remember it was warm as a hand in my curving palm; I remember the sweet, dazed smell of it.

Sean was troubled by the magpie's presence. After he'd had his tea, he went down to the rocks to fish up a gurnard for the dinner. I could see his bright hair there on the dull shore and his repeated glances back. When he returned with a cold red fish hooked to his finger by its gill, the magpie had vanished, leaving only the darkness of its occurrence in our heads.

And that was the last summer before the exodus. Frenchmen and Germans came by launch to negotiate for the houses, drawn by the future emptiness like vultures to a kill.

— No, we'll keep our houses so. We'll come back in the summers for the fishing.

Someone added: Sure and won't ye only want to build hotels and fancy roads. On *our* land, do ye mind.

I had my own idea of what would happen. In my mind's sad eye, I saw the fishermen return for one summer's work before they realized it was a dying vocation to farm the sea in the small boats of their ancestors. I saw the low houses lying empty and windbeaten year after year, windows breaking and the wind entering. There were curtains moving in the violated rooms and mice scuttling to their nests in the stuffing of chairs. I could smell the musty books still on the shelves and the mildewed linoleum curling from the floors. Barnacles claimed the quay. Stone byres lost their thatch and fell back to earth, in time only mounds of shore rock dislocated on the bony land. But I could say nothing, of course, having not even the tenuous right of a lichen to the island's geography or future.

The old men spent most of their waking hours staring to sea. Which changed, as seas do, almost hourly. It was as though they were committing to memory the physiology of their own cells and blood and the lost dream of Venus. There was the azure that a fine day could produce, and the coral strand of Ballyconneely, seen in the distance, made you think of the South Pacific you knew from the pages of *National Geographic*. Then there was the muddy cold that could only be the North Atlantic. And a deep glittery blue, waves white-capped and treacherous, and some days there was a horizon clearly delineated past Slyne Head.

– Now would ye not expect *that* to be the very end of the world?

– Aye, ye'd expect it all right. But tis a mirage, they say, and ye could go on for miles beyond that.

Cold water, and swimming things travelling the long miles to the banks of Newfoundland.

LAMENT FOR CHRISTY KING

THERE WAS A WEEK that summer when four men from Roundstone were lost on the water, practically waked in the days of their actual loss, then they were found afloat but dead-engined off the coast of Clare.

So of course there was great partying to be found in every pub at any hour of the day or night for two weeks after. One Sunday, after a hard week's fishing, we went to Clifden for the evening, ten or twelve islanders and myself rowing over to Eyrephort, bright-eyed in anticipation of good talk and drink.

— *Oy*, said the crippled man in Joyce's pub. The Roundstone people are blessed for this miracle (tipping back a pint of good stout). But tis the lifeboat people I'm in wonder of, looking for four days as they did and never finding a sight of the boatmen, though Patsy Joe will tell ye that the lifeboat passed within an arm's length of them. Makes a man think, does it not? They've put sailing boats into the air, made them fly. They've put people in them, good men like ourselves, lads, they've landed them on planets, brought 'em back again. But they couldn't find four men lost on the sea. Oy, as yer Aran man said, the world's a wonder, and a terror to our hearts.

We thought about that all right, sitting there in the big chairs your body could mould into, looking out at a few cars gliding down the wet street like whales. A murmur of voices at the bar, a clink of bottles, someone humming, the smell of porter and wet wool, pipe smoke; and the utter loveliness of whiskey whirling in glasses and reflecting off hands, deep gold and shot with light.

We rowed home that night, made lonely by the drink, and the oars were quietly creaking on their pins.

And then there was the week when the tinkers returned. I was riding Seamus's bicycle over the Sky Road, and there, like a weird and colourful apparition, was the same group of travellers, the same mare, and I'd not swear about the dogs but they looked the same, too, and if they were not (but cousins, no doubt), well, it really makes no difference.

– Ah, lass. Ye're still riding the same bicycle, I see, and we've the kettle on for the tea. Will ye have a cup?

– I took one. Thick as tar, and black this time, because Paddy Bourke had moved his herd to his brother's land at Aillebrack, and no one within miles had a freshened cow.

I looked as discreetly as I could at the various men of the menagerie to catch the eye of Christy. But he was not there.

– Did you have a good time in Sligo? Christy said you'd be going to the ceilis.

A few of the women looked at one another, then down. A youngish girl, twelve or thirteen and beautifully darkeyed, hair the colour of wild furze honey, said, Well, Sligo is all right now, but sure didn't Christy fall into a ditch on the way home from a dance, he'd many pints taken, and he slept in the reeds until dawn. When he woke, he'd a terrible cough, all raspy it was, and a few days later he died of the pneumonia.

An older woman, his mother I supposed, suddenly wailed to the sky for this wild son of the devil, *her* son, now cold and wormy in the ground: Oh, my grief! I've lost him surely. The other women silently blessed themselves, and one led the stricken wailer away.

I put down my cup, returned to my bicycle, moved away in the tarnished morning. Christy, you wretch, you leaver. Now that you've died, I wish I'd gone with you. What good are you to me or any woman now, you with your beautiful, breathtaking hands. How could anyone say: I've fallen in love with a tinker in his absence, I've killed him far away with my stupid infidelity. How could anyone say: I *wanted* the caravans, imagined the eerie paraffin lights and the twining limbs of the children, the wrath of a drunken father; I wanted to travel all the days of my life. Now I am stuck like a thorn in the pure body of a fisherman, my various lingering sadnesses a confusion to his soul.

> *At night when I go to my bed of slumber,*
> *With thoughts of my true love running in my mind,*
> *Well, I turn around to embrace my darling,*
> *Instead of gold sure tis brass I find . . .*

In the fairytale of my childhood, the ruined maiden

went forth from her father's house into the woodlands to live amongst the animals. In a dream, she'd be taught to make a cloak of stinging nettles, pounding and twisting the roots till she had lengths of a terrible fibre which she wove into a rough garment. She'd learn to feed all winter off berries with the partridges and deer. And in the spring a good prince would discover her hidden in an oak bole, and he'd fall in love with her swarthy religious face (she'd acquired a love for God through His creatures), her nettle-blistered hands (he'd kiss them), and he'd take her away on his white steed to a castle gorgeous with hangings and heraldry. Her sins would have been purified by cold, the penance of twigs in her wild hair and the rasping cloak on her arms. She'd have learned the mortification of wormwood, bitter and sorrowful, and she'd have learned patience in the cramped burrow of her woody home.

But where would I go, and who would have me? I'd wear my failures sheer as silk upon my shoulders, both an elegance and a falsity. The work of worms or of serpents.

✠ ✠ ✠

The government was taking its own sweet time in the completion of the houses, and the islanders were beginning to worry.

— T'would be a desperate winter if we were to have to spend it here. We're without doing the preparations that we usually know are for doing come summer.

— Aye, and isn't yer man to be found in Kelly's pub day and night, Flaherty, the one they say is in charge of the building?

I was always surprised at their thorough knowledge of the individual doings of the county, as isolated as they were. Who said what, owned what, married whom, had connections with the IRA.

A few literate men wrote to the councils and the newspapers, stating their cause in a terse, unnatural prose. The reply was a launch full of photographers and a journalist or two and even a documentary filmmaker; the result, pages of photographs in the nation's newspapers (men beaching a currach, the cottages, thin cattle, a few of the children peering big-eyed) and inspired paragraphs about the stark beauty of Inishbream and the betrayal of the islanders. Miceal would have not a thing to do with them, and they printed accounts of his reticence and his single statement: Would ye ever leave Heaven for Hell, I ask ye now?

For this was what it had come to mean. The promised land of the council plots, nearly a reality, seemed remote in the soft air of an island summer, however rainy, a tiny harbour all gentle with boats and fields lush with wild flowers hidden in the sharp sand-formed grass.

— But if we are to leave, we'd best to go soon. We do not fancy rowing load after load of belongings over the rough seas of November, do ye follow me? And there's no fodder for them ladeens to be eating (pointing to the remaining bullocks).

And in my own northern cottage, there were silent evenings in front of the fire. The wireless had worn down to a static drone, so we left it switched off except for the sea-area forecast, now unaccompanied by the dark bed of the night.

I cleared my throat. Sean, can we talk?

— What is it yer wanting to say?

— It's all different now, isn't it? Us, I mean. I'd like to leave, to go back to Canada where I belong. I'm not happy, and I think I must make you unhappy, too.

— Woman, I was expecting ye to bring that up. Do ye think I am blind and do not see ye pacing the island like a paddocked horse? And there is the talk I have heard. Ye was seen with that tinker. Some think that is why ye don't have a child. It is hard for a man to know he has not made his woman content, that she has had to go looking for another man and a tinker at that, a sly milk-stealing cur.

How could I begin to explain: It was never you, I never looked for him, he was there one day, and I was taken by his eyes, his mountainy smell. Or: It is that I am always watched when I walk, when I row out alone. I am expected to fail. There is always the shadow of a face behind those curtains or a figure in a doorway.

Instead, I said the usual things: I am sorry, I did not want to hurt you, believe me, forgive me. Then: Are you angry?

— Ah, I am thinking our marrying was a bad thing, a cursed thing from the beginning. And ye not a true

Catholic, how could ye know the bonds we expect? I think ye want to be at the fishing more than ye want to be a wife so. Ye must go back to Canada all right, but could ye wait until the move? It would seem more natural, like.

So the other women prepared for the move, lining trunks with newspaper and packing the china carefully, dusting the awful Kennedy glasses (resplendent with stars and stripes forever). They could be seen any time of the day wringing out linen, airing quilts and apprehensions over the stone walls. It seemed a lorry would meet the currachs on the beach and would deliver the things to the new houses, the lorry driver a cousin of someone, a man who would oblige for a night of pints in the town. The government provided money to buy large furnishings to replace what would never fit in the currachs: beds, dressers, etc. The few cattle that weren't sold in the summer fairs would swim across, towed on ropes behind the ark of possessions. The nets and pots would stay, piled in byres and unused rooms, waiting for the return of the fishermen, growing dry and warped with the salt of their exile.

There was a week when Peter conducted the sale of his pukaun, sailing to the town quay as weather or tides permitted, showing his boat silently to the sporty sailors who coveted the last of the island pukauns, the boat Peter's grandfather had built in the old way: laced ribs, measurements of body (length of an arm, distance between knuckles). Then he drank himself to a grim oblivion from his secret and nearly depleted supply of poteen, wailing a dirge to his lady boat on the rocks in front of his cottage. No one called to him to shut up or tried to prevent his drinking.

And I walked longer hours on the north end or gathered shells to keep: limpets *(they will always return to the scar they have made. It is like a home to them)*, cockles, the night-coloured mussels.

EPILOGUE

AND THE TRUTH of this story is: I did not wait for the move, did not help in any good way, have no idea of its real proceedings. I left. Went east by train like any tourist to Dublin, stayed in a poor hotel, my room above the bar and loud with "typical" evenings. There was a drama festival, cheap seats could be had in the gods, so I saw *The Tinker's Wedding*, saw the sweet ballet of the western world. I met an acquaintance in the Brazen Head, and as we sat drinking whiskey, the dog of a regular sniffed my boots, unworn since Inishbream.

— Have ye been in the fields then? It is that he smells cattle or wild birds. Moss and the like. He's not used to such smells.

— Yes, I have been in the fields.

There were days when I almost went back, when the city was rank with fish and I remembered the nets, still usable, when my eyes filled with the memory of soft gas lamps and mist.

But I took the boat-train to London, thinking: There at least I'll not be reminded. Walked through Hyde Park, the

Moore sculptures recumbent on every horizon, curved as a dolphin rib forgotten on a mantle. Finally I bought a ticket home.

The flight attendants will be serving hot canapés shortly. Please have your seats in the upright position. The usual crowd for economy class. The usual meals. Seats upholstered in purple, gaudy red, colours seldom if ever found in true nature. And the people as well. Maybe walking in the tamed park most cities have for a heart and recreation. Or else topped by hunter's orange and well armed against bears.

— A canapé, madam?

Serve me a beggar on horseback, a tinker in the grave. The odd thing about flying is the proximity of the moon. A pale occurrence in an unnatural sky. And him, maybe, watching. Ah, it's Christy, by the stars of God! I'd know his way of spitting and he astride the moon.

— Yes, please. And I'd like whiskey, too. Irish, if you have it. No ice.

Below I could see clouds for hours and hours and then, through an opening, mountains. Silvery threads of lost rivers, blinding lakes, power lines, slashes that could be ski runs. Animals, too, if I knew where to look.

It was evening as we approached Vancouver, city lights illuminating the tines of trees and the sea catching the end of the sun. Someone, my father, my brother, would be waiting to ferry me home over the wide gulf. If we were lucky, we'd see a trawler or gillnetter heading north for a salmon opening, the men warming their hands around mugs of strong coffee, their nets waiting to be thrown to the sea.

All my days on Inishbream were darkened by currachs and black sole, the twilights broken by children tossing their endless stones to the sea, taking up fragments of the island and closing the thin bones of their fingers around them, then casting them away.

When I remember my year, I'll say: *I was married to the boatman, his long oar alight with phosphorescence and his embrace bright with the scales of mackerel. I was never given a brown mug. Never, like Festy, did I discover a message in a bottle, never, like Agnes, did I grow a child in my womb, never knitted a gansey. My house grew lichens yellow as the sun, and snails crossed the threshold, reappearing out of thin air when I'd removed them one by blessed one.*

The grey geese circled Inishbream and the population fled, leaving their tables laid for another stranger to discover, leaving a brand of turf to burn away to cold ash. The currachs lay beached like dead whales on the mainland strand, the ribs splitting in the sun. There could be no burial, just the changing dunes of Eyrephort Strand, and no other way for a man to return.

Acknowledgements

Most writers are lucky to have one good editor in the course of bringing a book to light. I count myself blessed to have had two. Crispin Elsted's precise and poetic mind helped to shape *Inishbream* in its lovely Barbarian Press edition, and Laurel Boone's careful and caring eye further assisted me in refining the text. I am grateful to them both.

THERESA KISHKAN lives on the Sunshine Coast of British Columbia. She and her husband, John Pass, operate High Ground Press, which specializes in the letterpress printing and publishing of poetry broadsheets and chapbooks. Her work has appeared in journals on this continent and abroad, and a suite of her poems was set to music by the composer Steve Tittle. She has twice won Province of British Columbia Cultural Service awards.

Kishkan is the author of six poetry collections and a book of essays, *Red Laredo Boots*, that brings to life a landscape impregnated with history and memory. In 2000, her widely praised first novel, *Sisters of Grass*, announced the emergence of a major new writer of fiction.